The Tax Assassin

A Seth and Ava Mystery

ALSO BY
CLAUDIA HALL CHRISTIAN

THE DENVER CEREAL:
(DenverCereal.com)
The Denver Cereal
Celia's Puppies
Cascade
Cimarron
Black Forest
Fairplay
Gold Hill (late Fall, 2012)

ALEX THE FEY THRILLER SERIES:
(AlextheFey.com)
The Fey
Learning to Stand
Who I am
Lean on Me

THE QUEEN OF COOL
(TheQueenofCool.com)
The Queen of Cool

THE SETH AND AVA MYSTERIES
(SethandAvaMysteries.com)
The Tax Assassin

The Tax Assassin

A Seth and Ava Mystery

Claudia Hall Christian

Cook Street Publishing
Denver, CO

ISBN (*13 digits*) : 978-1-938057-08-3

Library of Congress: 2012919047

PUBLISHER'S NOTE:
This is a work of fiction. Names, characters, places and incidents either are the product of the author's imagination or are used fictitiously.

First edition © October, 2012
Cook Street Publishing
PO Box 18217
Denver, CO 80218

For the Silent Partner.

One

"So you think she's coming back?"

Seth O'Malley looked up from the ancient upright piano he was playing.

"You asked me the same thing last night," his friend and housekeeper, Maresol Tafoya said, as she leaned against the doorframe.

"I don't remember what you said." His fingers continued their dance along the keys, unleashing a familiar tune.

"Otch." She moved into the room to pick up a crystal tumbler sitting next to the couch. "You're drinking! Twenty years of sobriety gone! Just like that. The girl's only been gone twelve hours."

He felt his back burn from the heat of her glare. He

continued playing until he was forced to respond.

"Dale," Seth said of their resident handyman. "He was here for a while last night. Plus, it's Scotch. I hate Scotch. Smell it."

She held the glass to her nose and nodded.

"It's ten?" he asked.

"It's ten," she said.

"You're late for work," he said.

She shook her head at him. She'd been his housekeeper since he'd graduated from Eastman School of Music more than four decades ago. They were closer than family and more comfortable than lovers. She went to the small, built-in bar along the wall and washed the crystal tumbler. She set it in the cabinet before wiping down the sink and bar. Tidying the room, she folded his mother's hand-stitched quilt and laid it across the back of the leather couch.

"Well?" he continued playing.

"Do I think she's coming back?" Maresol kneeled down to sweep the ashes from the fireplace.

"Would you mind telling me again?" he asked.

"I think she's having a very difficult time," Maresol said. "She's had a lot of hard, horrible times that would break most young people. I understand why she wants to be with her mother now; so do you. She wouldn't have gone if you hadn't encouraged her."

"But?"

"Yes. I do think she's coming back to you, old man."

"Old man?" He smiled.

"You'll be fifty-nine in a few months," she said.

"And you?"

"Otch, don't be mean," she clucked and set up another fire in the fireplace. "Maybe you should start drinking again."

He laughed. Standing up, she put her hands on her hips to survey the small, wood-paneled room.

"To what do I owe the pleasure of your company?" He stopped playing and turned to look at her. She scowled at him. "You're right. I'm an ass. I'm sorry."

"You have a guest," she said.

"Who?" he asked.

"One of your war buddies," Maresol said. "He asked to speak with you in private, then had the nerve to ask if I was making rellenos for lunch."

He smiled.

"I wasn't planning to make rellenos for lunch." She gave him a sour look. He chuckled and she shook her head. "Should I send him down?"

"Who is it?"

"McArthur, McAudry," Maresol shook her head.

"McGinty?" Seth asked.

"Sure," Maresol said. Switching to Spanish, she added, "All you old white men look and sound the same to me."

Seth laughed.

"Go," Maresol said. "Wash up. You've been up all night, and you smell of worry."

"You think he'll care?"

"I care," she said. "I'll bring him down on the

elevator. With Ava gone, your puppy needs a walk. I set clean clothing for you in the bathroom."

Seth watched Maresol leave the room. His fingers itched to return to the quiet space provided by the song and this hand-me-down piano. He'd touched the keys for the first time when he was four years old and had written his first concerto right here when he was eight years old. He returned to the sanctuary of this piano whenever he could.

He grunted when he stood. His stiff joints were the only remnants of almost dying from First Responder's Toxin. He made a slow, stiff journey to the full bath he'd installed in his father's precious den. Five minutes, a brutally hot shower, and a fast shave later, he was playing the piano again.

He looked up to see Maresol holding the elbow of his old friend, McGinty. His hair and clothing were clean, but an indentation around the oxygen cannula in his nose and his unkempt fingernails told a tale of a long hospital stay. Seth stood to greet his friend. Maresol left the room to make chile rellenos.

"Before you ask," McGinty's voice came out in gasps. "I got the sarcoid like Mitch."

Seth nodded. His best friend, Mitch Delgado, died from sarcoidosis almost ten years ago.

"Rained Agent Orange on us," McGinty said. "Didn't it, Magic?"

"Rain?" Seth smiled. "The tunnels flooded with the stuff. I still taste it in my dreams."

"Nightmares. You ever go see the museum they made out of hell?"

"No."

The finality of Seth's 'No' spoke volumes. McGinty shuffled to the couch. As if he'd walked a long way, his eyes closed with relief when his ass hit the cushion. Seth sat on the piano bench and waited for his friend to collect himself. When he was ready, McGinty opened his eyes and looked around the room.

"How 'bout you, Magic?" McGinty asked. "Anything?"

"Nah," Seth said.

"We didn't call you Magic O'Malley for nothing," McGinty smiled, coughed, and closed his eyes again. His face took on a blueish cast. He waved his hand. "You can play."

"I'd rather talk," Seth said.

"Heard you had some hot, young girlfriend," McGinty opened his eyes to wiggle his eyebrows.

"She's taking a break from being my girlfriend," Seth said. "I wore her out."

McGinty coughed a laugh.

"Her name is Amelie," Seth said.

"Same as that song we used to hum when we were chasing VC in those damned tunnels?" McGinty chuckled.

"She's named after the song."

"I heard that song once when I was on an elevator," McGinty said. "No offense, but I had to get off the elevator. That song, in a small space? Brought too much back."

Seth waited. Eventually, McGinty would get to the point.

"I'm running out of time, Seth," McGinty said. "I

know I've only got a few months left. I can feel it in my bones."

McGinty nodded to Seth.

"I like that you don't try to talk me out of it," McGinty smiled. "You're a good friend."

"Just seen it before," Seth said.

"We've seen a lot of death, you and I," McGinty said. "How many years did you work homicide?"

"Fifteen?" Seth shrugged.

"That's right," McGinty said. "You and Mitch did a tour in Vice. You really out?"

"I'm on contract to the new chief, but I haven't started yet."

"Sounds cushy," McGinty said. "When you s'posed to start?"

"Why?" Seth gave McGinty a hard look. "While I appreciate the old man routine, and I know you're sick, I've known you, Harry McGinty, for a long, long time. You've never made a social call in your life. Why are you here?"

McGinty smirked and Seth chuckled.

"There are two things I'd like to do before I die," McGinty said. "I'd like to take Mary Ann on that cruise to Greece. You know, I promised I'd take her to Greece when we got married thirty-five years ago? Never did. I made the reservation on Monday. We're going at the end of the month."

"And the other thing?" Seth asked.

"I have this . . ."

"Case I'd like to solve," Seth said with him. "Of course."

McGinty smiled.

"Every old detective has a case he couldn't solve," Seth said. "They're like bones we can't stop chewing on."

"You still have one?" McGinty asked. "Heard you just solved that Saint Jude thing."

Seth nodded.

"Then you're bone free," McGinty said. "Old dog like you, you need a solid, unsolved case between your teeth to get the juices flowing again. And this is a doozy."

Seth smiled at the image, and his old friend laughed. His laugh became a cough. Seth got up to get him a glass of water.

"I wouldn't say no to some of that sixty-year-old Scotch you keep down here," McGinty gasped through breaths. "You pour, and I'll talk."

"Deal." Seth got up from the piano bench and went to the bar. He poured McGinty a few fingers of Scotch. "Ice?"

"Sure," McGinty said.

Seth got ice and a bottle of water from the small refrigerator he'd installed under the bar and brought McGinty the drink. He sat on the piano bench and watched his friend drink down the Scotch. When his glass was empty, Seth got the bottle.

"I forgot that you're trying to use up your father's Scotch," McGinty said.

"I still have more than a case," Seth said.

"It's good Scotch," McGinty smiled

"You were going to tell . . ."

"Yes, yes," McGinty waved at Seth's impatience.

"Why waste time with pleasantries when there's a murder on the line?"

Seth smiled.

"It's simple," McGinty said. "That's why."

"Simple, unsolved, and a doozy?"

"That's right," McGinty said.

"What is it?"

"Four individuals were killed in the summer of 1994 in Minneapolis. I'd just made sergeant and had a couple kids working under me. It was . . . a good year. But any year before this . . ." McGinty gestured to the portable oxygen tank. " . . . was a good year."

"Why 'individuals'?" Seth asked.

"I knew you'd catch that," McGinty said. "Two men; two women – one old; two middle aged; one young. Killed on different days of the week, in different areas of the city, with different weapons – knife, couple handguns; shotgun; but . . ."

"No M.O.," Seth took a battered manila folder from McGinty's outstretched hand.

"No," McGinty said. "At least one of these is considered solved. This guy, Frank Kolar. They charged the wife because she wanted a divorce and he wouldn't give it to her. There was some question of money missing from their account six or seven months prior to this incident. Her defense lawyer said he spent it on hookers and beer."

McGinty nodded.

"And?" Seth asked.

"She got off," McGinty said.

"And you don't think she did it?"

McGinty shook his head. Seth waited through a long, pregnant pause.

"Okay," McGinty said. "You're going to get there soon enough."

"Get where?"

"There's no link between these murders," McGinty said. "Or these."

He took a folder out of the inside pocket of his jacket and held it out. Seth took the folder and opened it.

"Four more murders," Seth said. "Omaha."

"Kansas City," McGinty threw another folder onto the sofa. "Jefferson City. Bismarck has five."

"Any more?" Seth looked to see what else McGinty was carrying.

"Not that I've found," McGinty shook his head. "But it wouldn't surprise me if there were more, a lot more."

"Why do you think these . . . are related?"

"Feeling," McGinty said. "That summer – 1994 – I couldn't shake the feeling they were related. Summer after? Omaha – four murders. You remember in those days, we didn't have the computers like we have now."

"And Omaha PD?"

"They charged a guy with a couple, but nothing stuck," McGinty said. "They got somebody in Jefferson City."

"But you don't think he did it?"

"He didn't do it," McGinty said.

"Serial killer?"

"Murder-for-hire," McGinty nodded. "That's what

I think. Kill a few in a city every summer and move on. Those smart FBI profilers can't see the connection, but to me? It's plain as day."

"The Kolar wife is guilty," Seth said.

"Or the husband," McGinty said. "He could have changed his mind. She said he came home in a rush that day and wouldn't leave her side."

"He got in the way," Seth said.

"Most people think I'm nuts," McGinty said.

"I know you're nuts," Seth said.

"Ain't that the truth?" McGinty's smile looked happy and worn, like a Jack O'Lantern that had dried out in the hot sun.

"But never about murder," Seth said.

"I was a good detective," McGinty said.

"You remember that day we were supposed to go down in Cu Chi and you said . . ."

"It's not a good day to be a rat." Remembering the young man he'd been, McGinty brightened. He sat up a little straighter. "You and Mitch were just kids. What were you. Sixteen?"

"Seventeen," Seth said. "You saved our lives."

"Was a long time ago," McGinty shrugged.

"Did you ever put a computer on this?" Seth asked.

"I found the other cases, if that's what you mean," McGinty said.

"But never put all the facts in a computer to see what came up," Seth said.

McGinty shook his head.

"What else should I know?" Seth asked.

"You mean you'll take a look at this?" McGinty asked.

"Of course," Seth nodded.

"Why?" McGinty chuckled.

"Because you deserve to die in peace," Seth smiled. "Plus, it gives me something to do."

"While your hot girlfriend is on a break?" McGinty asked.

Seth smiled.

"Come on," Seth said. "Let's get some rellenos."

Seth helped his old friend to his feet, and they made their way to the elevator.

"You'll keep me in the loop?" McGinty asked.

"When do you head back?" Seth asked.

"We're vacationing in Crested Butte for a week," McGinty said. "Mary Ann's at the art museum this morning."

"Do you have email?" Seth asked.

"Mary Ann does," McGinty said. "She's on that thing every day."

"Phone?"

McGinty nodded.

"Landline?"

"You mean one of those portable cancer causers?" McGinty asked. "No thank you. I prefer to get my cancer the good old-fashioned way – fighting for Uncle Sam."

He smiled and Seth chuckled.

"How 'bout this? I'll call you every evening," Seth said. "Until your cruise."

"You think you can solve this by the end of the

month?"

"I can try."

McGinty nodded and they got on the elevator. They rose to the first floor before McGinty said, "I sure hope you do."

"Why?" Seth asked. "Why this case?"

"The guy gets away with it," McGinty said. "Twenty, thirty, fifty . . . a hundred murders. He kills and walks away. Every time. He walks away. It . . . pisses me off."

As if on cue, the elevator doors opened to the first floor.

"It's about time," Maresol yelled from the kitchen. "Your rellenos are getting cold."

Seth nodded to McGinty and followed him out of the elevator.

|-||-|||-||-|||-||-|||-||-|||-||-|||-||-|||-||-|||

Two

He felt the bed shift before she was on him. He wrapped his arms around her warm body. She pushed his arms away. She pulled at the covers, ripped his T-shirt, and yanked on his boxer briefs. He opened his eyes to look at her. Her face was flushed as if she'd been running and her inch-long dark hair was wet with moisture. The slight sheen of moisture made her young, perfect skin glow. Her eyes saw only the intensity of her need.

They'd been through this before.

She didn't want to be held. She didn't want to be kissed. She didn't want to be stroked or loved or listened to. She wanted to feel something other than the numbness brought on by her own intense emotions. She wanted hard, fast release. She wanted what he could give her.

He gave her what he had. When he tried to shift her under him, she fought him. She wanted to be on top. She drove their exchange until they peaked in soundless passion and she had the release she'd come for. Panting, she dropped to his chest.

He pushed her away to look into her face. She gave him the embarrassed smile she always wore after these exchanges. She knew he loved her. She knew he didn't judge her. She was embarrassed by her own need.

"Stay here," he said.

He got up, grabbed a robe, and went to the kitchen, where he collected a Tupperware full of her favorite brownies and a glass of milk. She was showering when he got back to the room. He leaned his head into the bathroom. She waved for him to join her.

She didn't have to ask twice.

When they were done, he grabbed a towel and left her to the warm water. After release, she needed to wash her mind, body, and soul of the stain left by the remnants of her numbness and sorrow. More herself, she returned from the bedroom about a half hour later wrapped in a towel.

Dropping the towel, she slipped across the bed until her head rested on his chest. She allowed his arm to drop over her shoulder.

"Missed you today," he said.

Moisture from her eyes fell onto his bare chest. Angry with her own sorrow, she sat up and reached for a brownie and the milk. Tucking a foot under her, she bit into a brownie.

"I saw the stack of files," she said. "Did you start

work?"

"Old friend brought me something interesting," he shrugged.

"And the map?"

"Series of summer murders in one city, then moving onto the next city the next summer," he said. "I've called around. It's possible the murders span the country."

"Women? Serial killer?"

"My friend thinks murder-for-hire," Seth said. "I'll know more tomorrow when I hear from other departments."

"Sounds interesting."

"I found myself with some time on my hands, so I thought I'd take a look."

She grimaced.

"I haven't really dug in yet." He smiled to reassure her. "I'll have plenty to keep me busy while you're gone."

Her eyes filled with sorrow. Turning away from him, she ate her brownie and drank the milk.

"What happened today?" he asked.

"Feds came and took everything away."

Her voice was rich and deep, with the functional tonality of the baroque masters – Bach or Lully. He allowed her words to flow over him.

"My mom . . ."

Emotion caught her and for a moment she could only cry.

"They came – thirty, forty of them – in the morning, early. 4:45? 5? Like you said they would. I . . . let them in, and . . . they were like an infestation and, we . . .

had nowhere to go."

"Backyard?"

"The next-door neighbors rented their upstairs rooms to the news channels," she said. "We went out back this morning, only to discover our own images on television with jeering reporters announcing our shame. And . . . parties! You remember that nice Mormon boy, Craig?"

"Your high school boyfriend?"

"Six houses from my house. That's where he grew up; where his family lives," she shook her head. "You know what he did? He threw a party. There was a banner on his house that said, 'The sluts're getting what they deserve' with an 'i'."

She rolled her eyes.

"Nasty signs should have good grammar," Seth said.

"Exactly," she said. "If you're going to be nasty at least spell it correctly."

"Should be a law," he nodded. A corner of her mouth lifted in what might have been a smile. Her brow furrowed and she ate her brownie.

"I called him to ask him to take it down," she said and took a drink of milk. "You know what he said?"

"I can imagine."

"He said that I always thought I was too good for him." Her voice shifted in imitation of his, "'And all this time you were nothing but a whore in your father's stable. Is that why you wouldn't screw me? I didn't offer you enough dough.' In the background, everyone laughed. I . . ."

"Did you shoot him?"

"No," she smiled at the idea. "They took my gun

when they took my badge."

"Would you like me to shoot him?"

"Would you?" she smiled.

"Amelie," he said.

"No," she shook her head. Her voice echoed with desperation, "Call me Ava. Please."

He touched her tearstained face.

"I can't be Amelie Vivian Alvin anymore," she said. "My father stole our name, dirtied it with his . . . whores and johns and pimps and political pandering and . . . You know, Mom thinks he's dead. She keeps saying, 'Your father would never do this to us – to me. He must be dead.' She doesn't know he's in witness protection."

"Doesn't want to know?"

"I honestly think she doesn't know . . . and . . . they took everything she . . . we own."

"The Feds?"

"Her dresses, jewelry, furniture, our baby clothing . . . Anything they could sell," she whispered as if her words were too painful to hear out loud. "His clothing too, but who cares? Computers. My little sister Bella's school computer. My older sister, Éowyn? She's not a DA anymore."

"Your father got her the position at the DA the same way he got you the position at the forensics lab at Denver Police," Seth said.

"I found her curled up in a ball in her closet," she said. "Big bad Deputy DA Éowyn Alvin, who always had something nasty to say about everyone and everything, especially me, was crying her eyes out. She was crying so hard she couldn't leave the closet. She's lost her house and had to move home to live with Mom, and now this . . . They took her clothing, jewelry, computer, and . . . even her precious Blackberry! Bella was chucked from college. No money, no college. Her loans are part of the fraud case and . . ."

"And?"

"Everyone I grew up with, all of our neighbors, gathered around to cheer on the Feds. Even the Mandolyns. You know, the elderly couple who took us to the pool in the summer?" she asked. "Our neighbors . . . they pointed and stared and gossiped and drank. Like they knew we were . . . bad . . . all along. My mom thought some of these . . . people . . . were her best friends. She . . . It's like she's dead inside."

"No pitch forks?"

"No torches," she said. "At least until . . ."

She stopped talking and looked at him. Angry and embarrassed, she scooted away from him toward the end of the bed.

"Until what?" he asked.

She stopped moving. She sat on the far corner of the bed with her back to him.

"I used the money you gave me to put them up in a hotel downtown." She glanced at him. "You see, I'm your whore and . . ."

He slid across the bed to catch her before she began to sob. He rocked her slightly. When she was able to hear, he whispered: "Everything I have is yours."

"We're not married."

"Why *is* that?" He smiled.

"Because of all of this."

"Want to get married now? We could be in Vegas in an hour. We weren't supposed to leave for our honeymoon until tomorrow. We could still make it."

She smiled at him.

"We have a dress, a tux. The rings are in the safe downstairs. The flowers are still amazing. There's a fancy cake in the freezer. I bet I could whip up a celebration and . . ."

"I want to marry you when this crap is over," she smirked. "I'm only planning on getting married once. I want it to be big, fun, and memorable. I don't plan on changing husbands like underwear. Not like *some* people."

"That's low. I change my underwear much less than that!" He clutched his chest as if she'd stabbed him. "I divorced the crazy one. I think you'll remember that Bonita was killed by Saint Jude!"

For the briefest moment, even her eyes smiled and she looked like herself for the first time since her father's toxic waste had polluted every corner of her life.

"She doesn't know it's your money," Ava said.

"Who?"

"My mother," she said. "I told her it's money I got for coming up with the treatment protocol for the First Responder's Toxin."

"You got a hefty payout."

"That the Denver Police Department kept," she said. "But really, Seth, without your money, she, my sisters . . . The Feds took the beds! There's no place to sleep."

"They're tearing up the carpets tomorrow," Seth said.

"Why?"

"Looking for documents, audio recordings," Seth said. "He said he kept everything in a safe at the house. That's what they're looking for."

"God." Ava shook her head. "There's more?"

"Your father was at the DA's office before he was attorney general. He was in politics for more than thirty years."

"And dirty the whole time."

"The Feds think he's the tip of a very large iceberg," he said.

"Mom blames you," she said. "For all of this."

"Me?"

"Dad told her it was your fault," she said. "You were jealous because of... Saint Jude, I guess. You made up the lies that got Dad killed. That's what she says. And... that's what I mean! It's crazy town; she's lost it. When we got to the hotel, she... I was glad I got them separate rooms, because the moment her door closed, Mom collapsed. It took all of us to get her onto the bed and... Come dinner, she's up as if nothing happened. Face on, everything in place... We ate dinner at Sam's No. 3. I love that diner. Went there almost every day when I was a uniform, but my mother... she'd never been there. Kept saying it was 'quaint.' But where else are we going to go? They won't seat us at her usual restaurants. I tried."

Ava swallowed hard.

"I ran here. From downtown. I had to get out. I had to . . . see you and explain that . . ."

"Take what you need," he said. "If we run out, I'll write another movie score or . . . sell something."

"Sell something?"

"The house," Seth said. "I'm a little old to still be living in my father's monstrosity of a house."

"I thought it was Maresol's house," Ava smiled.

He held her close.

"I'm going to move them," she said. "Albuquerque, Las Vegas, some place smaller with a college so Bella can finish – any place away from here. Mom told me that she wants to start over, get her own job. I guess she was a paralegal."

"Have the Feds asked about your money?"

"Not yet," she said. "But I think they know about you and me. Plus, did you know they took all of the cars? Not mine, but my sisters' cars and my mother's. Gone. If you hadn't bought me the car, and Sandy . . . She had the receipt and . . ."

He leaned back to look into her face.

"Don't I have to talk to Sandy to get more money?" she asked.

He smiled. As part of his sobriety plan, Sandy, his eldest daughter, controlled his money. By the grace of God, and Sandy, he would never again have access to enough money to fuel his self-destructive habits.

"I'll call Sandy," he said.

"That's okay," Ava smiled. "She called midday. Told me about the car. The hotel was her idea. She's already called real estate agents in Las Vegas and Albuquerque to see about houses."

"Sounds like Sandy." Seth smiled at her. "What's your older sister going to do?"

"I don't know," Ava said. "She's . . . barely functioning. Our family name, status; it meant so much to her. Even when we were kids, she built a whole world around how we were State Attorney General Aaron Alvin's children and we . . ."

The horror of the day caught her again. She let out a small sob.

"Does he get to do this and just . . . walk away?" She clutched him.

"Looks that way," Seth said.

She began to cry in earnest and he pulled her to him. While sobs wracked her body, he rubbed her shoulder, kissed her hair, and whispered that he loved her. She cried for her mother, for her family, for her sisters, and finally for herself. The flood of sorrow rose and fell. When her sorrow was spent, she slept.

He closed his eyes for what seemed like a moment. When he opened them again, the late spring, predawn light was staring to brighten his second-floor, mullioned windows.

She was gone.

|-||-|||-||-|||-||-|||-||-|||-||-|||-||-|||-||-|||

THREE

Unsure what to do with himself, he took a shower. With the warm water beating on his head, he tried to retrieve the new piece of music he could feel growing inside him.

Nothing came.

He knew better than to force it, so he got dressed. He was pulling on his boots, when the murder-for-hire mystery drifted into his mind. Focused on the problem, he slipped down the wide oak stairwell to the kitchen where he'd left the files. He had downed two cups of coffee before he realized he had a problem.

He didn't have a place to work.

His father's eighty-five-year-old home was nearly four thousand square feet, plus the basement, in two stories. That didn't count the "carriage house," which contained a lap pool and two upstairs apartments. The house was not big by modern standards, but since his father's death, he'd lived here alone. It was too big for one man.

And he didn't have a space of his own.

Sure, he had a grand piano in the front sitting room, his upright piano sanctuary downstairs, and the front corner bedroom. But he'd always done his detecting in his office at the Denver Police Department. He'd learned from his first marriage to never bring work home; a lesson that stuck longer than the marriage.

There was no space for him to work here. He went to look for Dale.

He followed the smell of paint fumes until he found the young man standing in the awkward posture of a grown boy, not quite a man, in the middle of a small bedroom on the second floor. Hearing Seth come in, Dale turned and smiled. He had impossibly green eyes, straight white teeth, and brown hair that hung in his eyes. His smile held all the charm, beauty, and angst of youth.

He had been Ava's best friend Beth's fiancé. When Beth was brutally murdered, Seth brought Dale to home where the young man had lived ever since. In the last few months, Maresol had tasked him with painting the interior of the house.

"I saw Ava before she left," Dale said.

"Oh yeah?" Seth scowled at the freshly painted white walls.

"I asked her," Dale said.

Seth turned to look at Dale.

"You know, was she coming back?" Dale asked. "Or

was she some kind of runaway bride? She laughed. I think she's coming back."

Seth smiled.

"Do you think . . .?" Embarrassed, Dale started scraping the remnants of paint from the rolling pan.

"Do I think?"

"Do you think she knows?" Dale asked.

"Knows?"

"That I told that reporter about her dad," Dale said. "She's the only friend I have left; I mean, except for you, but you're really more like my surrogate dad or uncle or something and less like a buddy, I mean, we drink together or I drink and you play, and I'm not saying you're old or too old, at least not for Amelie. I just . . ."

Dale caught Seth's smile. He gave a self-conscious smile in return.

"Do you think she knows?" Dale asked.

"I think it's interesting that you believe you were the only one who called," Seth said. "I heard that someone called *Westword* about a week before a couple of other people called Barton Gaston directly. I've asked Barton how many and who called, but he wasn't going to reveal his sources, yada, yada, and all that."

"I feel . . . guilty," Dale said.

"You shouldn't," Seth said. "A lot of good people were set free, and a very bad man who lived without consequence was taken off the streets."

"But Amelie and her mom . . ."

"The truth always comes out, Dale," Seth said. "What's happening to them is a direct result of Alvin's actions, not yours. It's awful, but trust me – they're better off. Give them a few years. You'll see."

Dale nodded.

"Why are the walls white?" Seth asked. "I thought Maresol was sick of gringo walls that spoke to her like my father."

"Maresol isn't going to work in here," Dale said.

"Who is?"

"You. This is your new office," Dale said. "The furniture's downstairs. If you help, we can set it up. Maresol bought another computer so you don't have to use hers."

Seth smirked.

"You turn off the Telemundo stream when you use her computer. She wakes me up to get it running again. And," He switched into an exaggerated Hispanic accent. "If I have to cook and clean for the old man, I should at least be entertained."

Seth laughed.

"But one thing I don't understand," Dale said. "About Maresol, I mean."

"Only one?"

"Yeah right," Dale grinned. "But . . . isn't she from Denver?"

Seth nodded.

"Highland's right?"

Seth nodded.

"What's with the heavy accent?" Dale asked. "I mean, her family's been here like a hundred years. She sounds like she's an illegal."

"She grew up speaking Spanish," Seth said. "She

didn't speak 'gringo' until she started working here. You can imagine how her Spanish went over with my father."

"He was a real dick?"

"I don't think he realized that her family lived here long before our family fled the potato-famine," Seth laughed. "Wouldn't have occurred to him."

"Maresol?" Dale shook his head. "She's been . . . um . . . "

"Bitchy?" Seth smiled. "She's worried about me."

"Oh," Dale said. "I thought it was me."

"She gets that way when she's worried about you too," Seth said.

Dale chuckled.

"Did you get breakfast?" Seth asked. "Or, I guess, dinner?"

"Nah," Dale said. "I was going to help you get set up then go to bed."

"Why don't I make us something to eat while you clean up?" Seth asked. "We can eat, move in, and you can get to bed."

Dale nodded, and Seth left the room. He made quick work of pancakes, eggs, and some bacon for Dale. He was holding the bacon over the pan when Dale joined him. They ate in easy silence. Seth made another pot of coffee, and they started moving furniture.

Maresol had retrieved his long work desk from his office at the Denver Police office. Originally a mahogany barn door, he and Mitch had it made into a desk big enough for both of them. Ten years after Mitch's death, Seth still placed a chair across from him for his friend. This hundred-year-old house didn't have overhead lighting so Maresol had purchased a variety of desk and floor lamps. When they were done, the room was well lit and very Seth.

"Austere," Maresol said from the doorway. "Nice."

Dale scooted out from under the desk.

"Try it now," he said.

Seth clicked a few keys on the computer, and the Internet connection came up.

"Where is the rug?" Maresol asked.

"Rug?" Seth squinted at her.

He loved the look and feel of the hardwood; she loved the lower maintenance provided by floor rugs. She scowled at him. He pointed to a rolled up wool rug leaning against the wall. She made a point of rolling it out by herself. The rug created an almost perfect contrast between the rich maroon of his desk and the pale honey color of the pine floors. His little office now had a big desk, two chairs, lots of light, and a rug – Seth was ready to get to work.

"Dale will pick up a white board for you today," Maresol said. "We'll put it over there."

When Seth didn't respond, Dale and Maresol left him to his work. He was just wondering where he'd left his phone, when he saw his cell phone sitting in the middle of the doorway. He picked up the phone and began making calls.

Four

When he'd talked to as many detectives as he could, and left messages for the rest, he turned to email. He sent a vague email asking every police department in every medium-sized town across the United States if they had four unrelated gun deaths clustered over a summer. He counted on the fact that his name and reputation would encourage people to take him seriously. If that didn't work, he'd have to talk to the FBI.

Scowling at the idea of calling the FBI, he settled down to read the Xeroxed police files McGinty had left with him. He always found that a slow, careful read through any murder file told him everything he needed to know about the murder and the cops working the case. The scribbled notes and frayed pages of McGinty's files told the tale of a detail-oriented cop and a much worried over case.

Seth got up mid-afternoon for a cup of coffee. He found a note from Maresol saying that there was no food in the house. She had gone to the supermarket. He left a pot of coffee brewing and went for a swim.

The ritual of swimming laps was relatively new to him. He loved running, but his joints were in no condition to handle running right now. Maresol had fixed and filled the pool, and practically pushed him in. He wasn't a very good swimmer compared to Ava's smooth strokes. But he enjoyed the silent, rhythmic press of one stroke after another.

Today, he focused on letting the details of the case – the *who*'s, the *why*'s, and the *where*'s – float away so that a pattern might appear. Unable to find one, he finished his laps and took his medically-prescribed fifteen minutes in the infrared sauna. A quick shower, and he was back in the kitchen drinking a cup of coffee when Maresol came in.

"It's decaf," he said to her disapproving look.

"You're drinking my decaf?" Maresol swore at him in Spanish.

He set his cup down and hugged her.

"Everything is really all right," he said.

"I worry about you," she said.

"I know," he said. "I'm going to be all right. I have this case and . . ."

The doorbell rang. They heard Dale jog down the stairs to answer the door.

"Visitors," Seth said. "You know how I love visitors."

She chuckled at him.

"You going to be okay this weekend?" Maresol asked.

"I am," he said. "I'll work, swim, and play my piano. If I get bored, I'll go play at Charlie Brown's or hang out with Sandy's kids. Don't worry about me."

She nodded. Hearing voices in the entryway, she patted his shoulder and went to see what was going on. He finished his coffee. He looked up to see two graying men wearing wrinkled sports coats, donut-induced paunches, and bad hair cuts standing in the doorway. Their worn cowboy boots, shiny belt buckles, and broad mustaches planted them firmly in the Western US. The identical service revolvers sticking out of their side holsters made them cops.

"Coffee?" Seth asked the police detectives.

"Sure," the older man said. "You O'Malley?"

Nodding, Seth poured two cups and set out a carton of cream. Maresol gave Seth a Tupperware of chocolate chip cookies. He nodded toward the door. The men followed him out of the kitchen and started up the stairs.

"Jeez, I heard you were loaded, but this place is gorgeous," the taller man said.

"It was my father's," Seth said.

"Your poppa had money?" the other detective asked.

"Just enough to sign a mortgage on the place," Seth gestured to the restroom. "You look like you've had a long drive. I'm two doors down."

The taller detective scooted into the bathroom.

"There's another one down the hall."

Seth pointed to the restroom next to Dale's bedroom. The other detective went down the hall. In his new office, Seth found that Dale had mounted a large white board on the wall while he was swimming. He'd even left non-smell, dry erase pens. He could almost hear Maresol instruct Dale not to the get the old man high. He smiled, and the taller detective ambled into the room.

"Wyatt Bodie." The taller detective held out his hand for Seth to shake. "My partner's Gage Markleman. We're from . . ."

"Salt Lake?"

"Casper."

Detective Bodie smiled without making his mustache move. Seth was about to ask about it when Detective Markleman came in. He shook Seth's hand.

"Sorry, I just moved in here today," Seth said. "I didn't think of . . ."

Dale stood in the doorway with an additional chair. Smiling, Seth took the chair from him and went back in the room.

"This is good coffee," Detective Markleman said. "Any chance of getting dinner?"

"Who is your captain?" Seth asked.

"Shepperson," Detective Bodie smiled.

"Told you about Maresol?"

The detectives laughed.

"Shep has a deep fondness for Maresol," Seth laughed.

"He told us," Detective Markleman said. Imitating his captain, he said, "Drive fast and you'll get the best dinner you've had in your entire life by the most amazing woman."

Seth laughed. As if on cue, Maresol appeared in the doorway.

"Are you staying for dinner?" she asked.

"They work for Shep," Seth said.

"Oh good Lord," she left without another word.

Seth laughed.

"What can I do for you?" Seth asked.

"We saw your email this morning," Detective Bodie said. "You probably heard we had some trouble last summer."

Seth shook his head.

"That's right," Detective Markleman said. "You were involved in that Saint Jude thing. Didn't you get the First Responders?"

Seth nodded.

"Sounded bad," Detective Markleman said. "I heard you could see and hear, but not move. That right?"

Seth nodded.

"And anything they did to save you would have killed you?"

"That's about it," Seth said.

The detectives shook their heads.

"So, I missed some trouble in Casper?" Seth asked.

"We had a weird situation," Detective Markleman said.

"One of the state representatives was shot, killed, in

Casper," Detective Bodie said. "Looked like a hunting accident."

"Hunting on a private reserve," Detective Markleman added.

"Shot while he was out," Detective Bodie said.

"It happens," Seth said. "Did he die?"

"Clean shot," Detective Bodie said. "Straight through the heart."

"The weird thing was . . ." Detective Markleman and Detective Bodie shared a look.

"What was that?" Seth asked.

"We took a lot of shit for this last summer," Detective Bodie said. "We wouldn't be here if the captain hadn't ordered us to come. Now here we are and . . ."

"We debated how much to tell you the whole way down, because I'll tell you, Criminal Investigations thinks we're nuts."

"Okay," Seth said. "What was the weird thing? Start from the beginning. Feel free to repeat yourself."

Detective Markleman nodded to his partner for him to set up the case.

"The representative was shot while he was out hunting elk on a private reserve," Detective Bodie said. "That's not a big deal. I'd say it's not a common outcome from those trips, but hell, the vice-president shot his friend on a hunting trip."

"It happens," Seth said.

"Right," Detective Bodie said. "Almost an exact match to their ammo – same weapon, same reload. Forensics even says it's similar enough lead. Tire weights, most likely."

"But?"

"He was shot with a hollow point," Detective Bodie said. "They didn't load hollow points. Wyoming CI says the hollow point musta got mixed in by accident."

"It happens," Seth repeated.

"Even the owner of the ranch said it's possible."

"Anything's possible," Seth said. "Doesn't mean it happened."

"Exactly," Detective Bodie said.

"Find any brass?"

"No," Detective Bodie said. "They weren't experienced hunters."

"They shot multiple times," Seth said.

"Every mark," Detective Markleman nodded.

"If the shooter was from the hunting party, we should have the brass," Detective Bodie said. "We found bupkis. Perfect shot, no brass. We figure it's got to be military, CIA, DHS, or something. Official word is *no*."

"There are a lot of vets in Wyoming," Detective Markleman said. "Those kids get home from the Middle East and want to hide some place they don't have to deal with too many people. Wyoming is perfect for them."

"Catch anyone?"

"The captain liked a guy for it but . . ." Detective Bodie said.

"Shepperson's a good cop," Seth said. "If he thought . . ."

"Even he said he was grasping at straws," Detective Markleman said.

Seth nodded.

"It wouldn't be as weird except that three other people were killed in the county last summer," Detective Bodie said.

"Same M.O. ?" Seth asked.

"No," Detective Markleman said. "Different weapons, different situations; almost every single detail about these crimes is different."

"Were they shot with the same precision?" Seth asked.

"No," Detective Bodie said. "The shooter in the representative's killing was clearly skilled. But the rest? Most looked like accidents."

"Or suicides," Detective Markleman added.

"But they were all shot with hollow points," Seth said.

"One hanging," Detective Markleman said. "Ruled a possible suicide with an emphasis on *possible*."

"No brass," Detective Bodie said.

"Did you bring the files and evidence?" Seth asked.

"It's in the trunk," Detective Markleman said.

Seth nodded. Detective Bodie got up and left the room.

"What do you think, O'Malley?" Detective Markleman asked.

"I'm not sure," Seth said. He picked up a black dry-erase marker and wrote on his new white board:

HOLLOW POINT

NO BRASS

RELOADED ROUNDS

TIRE WEIGHT LEAD

NO M.O.

VARIETY OF WEAPONS

He turned to the detective.

"Three firearms, one hanging?" Seth asked.

"Yep," Detective Markleman said.

"Any other suicides? Weird deaths?"

"Slit wrists," Detective Markleman said. "Cut her arm clean off. Contentious divorce; a couple of kids; husband an asshole. You know the drill."

Seth put a dash at the end of "Variety of weapons" and added "Firearms, one knife (suicide)."

"What about the rope?" Detective Markleman asked.

"I doubt it was related," Seth said. "That doesn't mean it's not murder. It's just that murder-for-hire usually sticks with a set of services. These are the characteristics of those murders."

Seth pointed to the stack of McGinty's files on his desk.

"There's more?" Detective Markleman asked.

"There's a lot more," Detective Bodie said. He came

in carrying an evidence box. He gestured to the hallway, "These guys were just getting out of their car when I got out there."

Five

"Cheyenne?" Seth asked.

"Rapid City Sheriffs, sir," a woman's voice said from the hallway.

"There's more?" Seth asked.

"Detective O'Malley?" A young man with ragged hair and a stained tie stuck his head in the room. "We're here from Wichita. We got your email . . ."

"So did we," a voice came from the hallway.

"Say, you wouldn't happen to be Maresol, would you?" a different voice asked from the hallway. "Our captain told us you were the best cook this side of the Mississippi. We came a long way. Would it be too much trouble . . .?"

Maresol threw up her hands and retreated to the

kitchen.

The police detectives kept coming.

Dale had just closed the front door when detectives from Scottsbluff, Nebraska knocked. A few hours later, detectives from Provo, Utah and Lubbock, Texas arrived. The detectives told the same tale of murder and asked for the same reward – dinner by Maresol.

After securing everyone's handguns, Seth broke out the alcohol they'd bought for the wedding reception. He recruited Dale to play bartender. When he went to check on Maresol, she was standing in the middle of the kitchen talking to herself in Spanish. He slipped out before she noticed him and went to the chest freezer in the basement. He took out the enchiladas, taquitos, and tamales originally destined for the reception dinner and carried them to the kitchen counter.

"They won't like it," Maresol said. "It won't be special enough, famous enough."

"They'll love it. This is great food. Just warm it up and add some cheese. It will be perfect."

"But . . ."

"I am the *master* in this house," Seth said. "This is what *I* want."

He ducked to miss the coffee mug she threw at him. The mug shattered against the cabinets behind him. He scooted out the door when she picked up a kitchen knife. When he peeked in a half hour later, she was singing along to the cumbia music blaring from her computer. She cast him a sly smile. He shrugged and retreated to the party.

A couple of bottles in, a detective attempted to

"help" Maresol in the kitchen. Before Seth could head him off at the pass, the detective was scooting out of the kitchen like his pants were on fire.

"She likes to work alone," Seth said.

Seth patted his back and gave him a beer to calm his nerves. Seth leaned into the kitchen and Maresol gave him a dark look. Seth smiled and closed the swinging door.

A man and woman walked toward him.

"The bartender said there's a hot tub?" a young man from Lincoln said.

The man gave a quick look to the young detective from Utah. She bat her blue eyes at him. Seth moved aside to send them through the kitchen, then thought better of it. He escorted them down the hall off the dining room and pointed to the carriage house. A couple women sat down in the chase loungers on the patio. Seth lit the chimenea so they would be warm and returned to the party.

Seth refreshed drinks, laughed at stories, and in general kept the party light. A detective from Scottsbluff was holding court with a long improbable story about a girl, a tall Native American shaman, and a coyote when Dale called Seth to the door.

Ava, her sisters, and her mother standing in the entryway.

"Welcome!" Seth said.

"We had nowhere to go," Ava said. "The press found us at the hotel and . . . I . . ."

Ava bit her lip to keep from crying. If they'd been alone, he would have held her. Given that her mother hated him, he caught her hand and turned to her mother.

"You are more than welcome here," Seth said. "A few detectives came from around the West to talk about a case. Maresol was just about to serve dinner. Please come in and make yourselves at home."

"Amelie told us about the wedding and the money; how you've helped us every step of the way," Ava's mother, Vivian Alvin, said. "I'm . . . sorry. That's all. After that reporter called our suite to warn us, my daughter corrected my impression that you had called *Westword*. The reporter said he'd promised you that he would take care of us, protect us from scrutiny, and he has; he truly has. This whole ordeal could have been a lot worse. And . . . I've been wrong, Seth. I hope you can forgive my pride and . . ."

"Of course," Seth held out his arms and hugged her. "You're welcome here for as long as you need – as long as it takes. We have plenty of space, certainly. And tonight, we have plenty of food. Please come in and join the party."

"Come help me, girls," Maresol said to Ava and her sisters. Seth raised his eyebrows in surprise. She shook her head as if he was the impossible one. "We have these hungry coppers to feed."

Relieved to have something concrete to do, Ava and her sisters were moving into the kitchen to help Maresol, when a man with a bushy white mustache to match his white cowboy hat said, "Vivian?"

"Jeb?" Ava's mother's hand self consciously touched her hair.

"Vivian Bell?" he asked. "Well, I'll be goldarned."

"Jeb Elliott. What are you doing here?" Vivian smiled.

"Came to talk to O'Malley about some trouble we had a few summers ago," Jeb said. "I'm the Pennington County Sheriff now. I have my very own office in Rapid City."

"And Patricia?"

"My Patty passed... Gosh, I guess it's been five years," Jeb said.

"I'm so sorry," Vivian said.

"Breast cancer. It was a relief for both of us at the end," Jeb said.

"My mother suffered like that, too," Vivian said. "Horrible."

"It's hard when good people are called to suffer so much," Jeb said "I heard about your... trouble. Golly, Viv. What the heck is going on in the world when a man gets caught up in all of that unsavory business?"

"I have no idea." Ava's mother looked down to cover her pain and humiliation.

"Well how could you?" Jeb glanced at Seth. "You must be here to see O'Malley? He's always escortin' the most lovely woman in the room."

"No," Vivian chuckled and shook her head. "I'm lucky he doesn't throw me out. I haven't been exactly civil."

"I bet," Jeb said. "Anybody who's going through what you are isn't going to be exactly civil. Terrible business."

"Awful," Seth said.

"I saw you hugging, and I just assumed you were..." Jeb looked at Seth, who shook his head. "You're certainly the most attractive woman in this room."

"He's marrying my daughter," Vivian said. "My *twenty-three* year-old daughter."

Jeb glanced at Ava, and she gave him a little wave.

"I can't say I'm not relieved," Jeb said. "Come on, Viv. Let's get you something to drink."

Jeb took Vivian's elbow and guided her past her stunned daughters and into the dining room. Seth shot an amused look at Ava and she wiggled her eyebrows.

"Good for her," Maresol said. "Now, come along, girls. We have plenty to do."

Once in the kitchen, Maresol assessed Ava and her sisters.

"Why don't you round up the detectives outside?" Maresol asked Éowyn, Ava's eldest sister. "There's a couple in the hot tub. You'd do well to make sure they know you're coming."

Relieved to have some non-cooking thing to do, Éowyn followed Maresol's finger and went out the sliding door to the backyard.

"Off you go," Maresol placed a tray of enchiladas in Ava's younger sister Bella's arms. "Don't let those old goats give you any trouble either."

Bella nodded and carried the enchiladas out. Maresol hugged Ava.

"How are you, dear?" Maresol asked.

"Is this my reception?" Ava's expression was neutral but her eyes echoed her desperate heartbreak.

"The *master* of the house *ordered* me to use this food from the freezer," Maresol said.

"Talking to yourself again?" Ava smiled.

Maresol laughed and hugged Ava again.

"Don't worry," Maresol said. "When we get you married, your reception will be perfect in every way. Trust me. We'll have a wonderful time."

"I love your confidence," Ava sighed.

"I am the master of the house," Maresol said.

Ava laughed. Seeing her little sister, Ava straightened her face back to neutral. Maresol gave Bella the taquito platter and she left the room. Éowyn came through the kitchen with the female detectives.

"Where are the others?" Maresol asked.

"Finishing up," Éowyn said. "I didn't want to . . ."

Maresol gave her a hard look and stomped out the sliding door. Éowyn and Ava heard Maresol tell the detectives to "get dressed and stop acting like horny teenagers." Éowyn glanced at Ava.

"She's . . ." Éowyn started.

"Amazing, isn't she?" Ava smiled.

Éowyn nodded. Maresol smiled when she came back in the house.

"Detectives are such children," Maresol said. "They are all like that."

Unsure of how to respond, Éowyn and Ava nodded.

"Is your family staying tonight?" Maresol asked.

"Do we have space for my sisters and mother?" Ava asked.

"We'll make space," Maresol said. She went to the doorway and waved Seth into the kitchen. Seth stuck his head in. "We should give Ava's mother your bedroom, yes?"

"Sure," Seth said. "Ava and I can sleep downstairs. We've done that often enough."

He smiled at Ava and she blushed.

"Then go change the sheets," Maresol said.

Laughing, Seth left the kitchen. When he returned, the party was in full pitch. He watched Dale lean over to say something in Ava's ear. Her face flashed with surprise, and her eyes welled with tears. She hugged him. Dale must have told her that he'd called *Westword* about her father. Seth smiled. Ava had responded like he knew she would – her friend, Dale, was more important to her than the secrets and lies that caused this transition in her life.

Feeling his eyes, she looked up and smiled at him. He tried to move in her direction, but was confronted by a detective who wanted to talk to him about investing in some prime "re-eel 'state" just outside of Shallowater, Texas. While he continued his pitch, Seth tried to imagine what could possibly be considered "prime" about the incessant hot, sandy wind of Lubbock, Texas. Rather than ask, he smiled and tried to slip away. By the time Seth sloughed off the detective, Ava was deep in a conversation with her sister, Éowyn.

Seth looked around the room. Jeb Elliot leaned in to talk to Ava's mother Vivian. A few of the men were making eyes with the female detectives. Ava's younger sister, Bella, was blushing at something the ragged haired detective from Wichita had said. Seth even noticed a few furtive glances between partners. As the alcohol and great food continued to flow, love was definitely in the air.

"We're going to have to sterilize the hot tub,"

Maresol said. "Detectives are such pigs."

"They are," he said.

Seth put his arm over her shoulder. They watched the party for a moment.

"You think I should make a run to the drug store?" Seth nodded toward the room. "Looks like they could use a box or two of condoms."

"Maybe a case," Maresol laughed.

She kissed his cheek and left him to fend for himself. Seth's eyes cast about the room for Ava. She was trapped in a corner by an intense detective. Seth tried to rescue her, but was waylaid by a woman looking for a charger for her phone. He'd just set her up with a charger when he saw that Ava had shaken off the detective. She winked at Seth and he moved in her direction.

He was stopped by an old Army friend. The detective was drunk and weeping. With the help of Dale, Seth navigated the man to one of the downstairs bedrooms and sat with him while he cried for all he'd done and all he'd lost. By the time Seth got him settled, the crowd had thinned and the hard drinkers were setting up a game of poker.

He took Ava's hand and slipped down the back stairs to the basement.

Six

When Ava ducked into the bathroom, Seth unlocked his piano sanctuary, lit the fire, and sat down at his upright piano. His fingers were moving across the keyboard, when he heard someone at the door. He looked up to see Bella.

"I heard the music and . . . everyone's mostly gone to bed." She took a step into the room. "Where's Amelie?"

"She's soaking in the bath," Seth nodded his head in the direction of the bathroom. "There's a big bathroom down here. She can soak for hours."

Bella nodded and took another step into the room. She was twenty-one years old, and almost done with college. Tonight, Ava's little sister looked very young and very frightened.

"Have a seat," Seth said. "I can get Amelie or . . ."

"No, that's okay," Bella said.

"Would you like some Scotch?"

She looked disgusted. Seth laughed.

"My thoughts exactly," Seth said. "I think there's some wine down here. I bet Ava would like some too."

He went to the storage room where Maresol kept the wine and found a Shiraz that Ava liked. When he came back into his sanctuary, Ava's sister was standing by the fireplace. She jerked with surprise when he came in.

"Sorry," he said.

"Oh," she said. "That's all right. I'm a little . . ."

"Upset," Seth said.

The girl nodded. Seth found a pair of wine glasses and poured her a glass of the Shiraz. Bella took her glass and sat down in the old leather chair. She seemed lost in thought, so Seth began to play. He'd almost forgotten she was there when she spoke.

"We used to be so close," Bella said. "Really close. My sisters and I. . . . Éowyn . . . And Amelie. I didn't know . . . about you. This. I look around . . . and this is Amelie's dream life. It's what she always wanted. I mean, not exactly this, but . . . a hot, smart guy who is comfortable with himself; a big, old house; a cozy life on a nice street; even the dog . . ."

"And you?" Seth asked. "What do you want?"

"I . . ." Bella shook her head. "Dad and I were close. I was his favorite."

Seth stopped playing. He turned around to look at Bella.

"You knew about . . . everything," Seth said.

Bella nodded. As if it held fascinating detail, she focused her attention on her wine glass.

"I didn't know it was a secret," Bella said. "I mean, I didn't like it but . . . I thought Mom knew. I thought she knew. I thought . . . And now Dad's gone to who knows where, and Mom . . . and . . ."

Bella broke down. He looked up to see his nine-month old chocolate Labrador puppy, Clara, fly into the room with Ava, clad in a light blue fluffy robe, on her tail. Ava stopped short when she saw her sister crying. She looked at Seth, and then kneeled down to hug the girl. Clara looked at the women, and then at Seth. The dog hopped onto the leather couch in the corner just behind him.

He played the piano while the sisters talked and the dog slept. He looked up when Ava leaned down to kiss him. She poured herself a glass of wine, refilled her sister's glass, and sat down on the arm of Bella's chair.

"This is Seth's inner sanctuary," Ava said. "Not many people have been here."

"I feel honored," Bella said. "Um, you asked what I wanted?"

Still playing the piano, Seth nodded.

"I want everything back the way it was," Bella said. "But, not back the way it was."

"Change is hard," Seth said. He kept playing because he wanted to, and because it helped keep the mood in the room light.

"Yeah," Bella said. "Three months ago, I was thinking about doing a semester abroad. You know, going to Ireland or France or somewhere cool. I'd come back only to graduate. Then this happened and . . ."

"I lost my job," Ava said. "Éowyn too."

"And Mom," Bella said. "I used to read *People* magazine and stuff like that online. Now that we're in those magazines and . . . They're like . . . vultures."

"Maggots," Ava said. "Feeding off dead things."

"Dead," Bella said. "Like us."

"They're feeding off your old life," Seth said. "Not you."

"Let them have it," Ava put her arm around her sister. "While they're feasting on the ruins, we'll build a new one."

"Like what?" Bella smiled at her sister.

"Like what do you want?" Ava smiled.

Bella looked at her sister, and then at Seth.

"You guys are really perfect for each other," she said.

"We think so," Ava said.

Seth stopped playing and turned around.

"Just because you knew about your dad and his activities, doesn't mean there was anything you could have done about it," Seth said.

Shocked, Bella's mouth fell open. She stared at Seth.

"But . . ."

"He told you because he knew you couldn't do anything," Ava said. "He arranged the forensics lab for me, and the DA's position for Éowyn, so if we ever learned about his business, we'd have too much to lose to tell anyone."

Surprised, Bella stared at Ava and then glanced at Seth. Seth nodded.

"I feel awful," Bella said.

"Don't," Ava shrugged. "We're young, smart, and well educated. Lots of people start over from worse spots. We can do anything we want to in this life. What do you want to do?"

"I'd like to go to France, or maybe Ireland," Bella smiled. "But how can I do that?"

"We can send you there," Seth said. "We planned on helping your mother, you, and Éowyn get back on track. Why don't you research what and where?"

"Good idea," Ava said. "Present it like a project: where you want to go; why you want to go there; and what you think you'll learn."

"I know a few people who work at the Sorbonne," Seth said. "You could go in January."

"How would I pay you back?"

"I like that you want to," Seth said. "But you don't have to."

"Figure it out in your project," Ava said. "Let us know."

"Why would you do that, when I didn't even . . .?"

"Because we can," Seth said. "Because we're family."

Ava glanced at him. He smiled to assure her.

"We all need help sometimes," Seth said.

"I hope to get Mom settled somewhere," Ava turned to her sister and smiled. "Looks like it might be Rapid City. Didn't she seem . . .?"

"Do you think they . . .?" Bella giggled.

"I don't want to know," Ava laughed.

Seth turned around to play the piano again. After a while, Bella got up to take a bath, and sometime later she leaned in the door to say she was off to bed. When she was gone, he closed the door to the piano room.

He joined Ava in the nest of blankets and pillows by the fire. She rolled over to him when he touched her back, but didn't wake. He kissed the top of her head and fell asleep.

When he woke, she and the puppy were gone again. He took a shower and wandered upstairs to see who had survived the previous night's party. He found Ava sitting in the kitchen drinking coffee and looking at the case files. He watched the puppy, Clara, chase a ball in the backyard.

"Hey," he leaned over to kiss her.

"Hey."

"I hope you don't mind," Ava gestured toward the files. "I had to look."

"Of course you did," Seth smirked at her.

"You know I trained in forensics at the FBI, right?"

"I remember."

"Right," Ava said. "When I came back to Denver, I did a couple of weeks at the CBI before going to Denver PD."

"Okay." Not sure what she was talking about, he poured and drank a cup of coffee.

"There's a case just like what you're working on," Ava said. "Brady, Bosley, Bradley something like that. Male; twenty-nine years old."

"In Timbuktu?" He poured the last cup of coffee and made another pot of coffee.

"Southeastern Colorado," Ava said. "Small town outside of Trinidad."

"Really?" Seth shrugged. "Why didn't the PD come to the party last night? I feel . . . slighted."

He held his heart, and Ava smiled at his antics.

"It happened in 1913," Ava said. "Tax agent gunned down while making the rounds. Never solved."

"Sounds fascinating," Seth raised his eyebrows.

"Sounds crazy," Ava said. "We got that grant from the Feds to solve old cases with new science. I was on a team that worked the tax agent's case. I'm sure our report is in the system."

"What'd you find?"

"What you have – reloaded round, firearm," Ava said. "If there was brass, which is unlikely, it didn't survive the years in the evidence warehouse."

"Basically nothing."

"Except . . ." She gave him a coy smile.

"Except?"

"The gunpowder was unusual," Ava said. "Made with cottonwood charcoal. We figured the killer made it himself because that's what most people did in 1913. Cottonwood charcoal gunpowder was also a favorite of the Confederate States. The tax agent was from Massachusetts, a Union state. We postulated that maybe the killing was about some unresolved business from the war."

"Colorado was a Union territory," Seth said. "So was New Mexico."

"Yes, but Texas was a part of the Confederacy," Ava said. "Texas isn't very far from where the tax agent was killed, especially if you have unresolved business."

He smiled at the interest and intelligence in her face. She took his smile as encouragement to continue.

"It's about a thousand miles from Palmito Beach, where the last battle of the Civil War was fought, to where this agent was killed," Ava said.

"A thousand miles isn't much ground to cover in forty-eight years," Seth said. When he fell silent, she waited for him to finish thinking. He looked up at her and said, "That's interesting."

"Of course, most gunpowder is manufactured now and, surprisingly, or at least I was surprised to learn that the method hasn't changed much since gunpowder was invented."

"Sulfur, charcoal and potassium nitrate or salt peter," Seth said.

"Right," Ava smiled. "How did you know?"

"My elder brother Saul used to make it when we were kids," Seth said. "Made his own fireworks. Very dangerous. Very fun. Used to scare my little brother Silas to death."

"I bet," Ava smiled.

He smiled at her smile. It was nice, if even just for a moment, that things felt normal. He touched her back to encourage her to continue.

"I used the spect on the sample we had from 1913."

"Oh yea?" Seth poured a cup of coffee from the new pot and offered some to her. She shook her head.

"That's how we found the cottonwood char," Ava said. "From the spect readout. Well, and the sulfur. But sulfur's pretty easy to come by here in Colorado. There's a lot at any hot springs. Pagosa's not too far from there and . . ."

The way Seth nodded, she knew he was ready for her to get to the point.

"There's a spect scan in one of your files upstairs," Ava said. "Your friend McGinty had it done a few years ago. Probably begged or bartered for someone to do it."

"The spect matches the one you ran from the 1913 case?" Seth asked.

"I don't have it in front of me, but I'd say it's close," Ava said. "I'd have to see our scan to be sure, but I'm pretty sure McGinty's 1995 murders match the spect signature of the case in southeastern Colorado."

"From 1913?" Seth asked.

Ava nodded. Seth fell silent. He refilled her cup without asking and set the pot down. She smiled at his mistake; he was too lost in thought to notice.

"What?" she asked when she couldn't stand waiting any longer.

"Assuming your 1913 case is the first, you're looking at a little less than a hundred years," Seth said. "At four a summer, you're talking . . ."

"Four hundred murders," Ava said.

"Good Lord."

|-||-|||-||-|||-||-|||-||-|||-||-|||-||-|||-||-|||

Seven

Seth nodded to the security guard sitting at the entrance to the Denver Central Library. He looked around the main lobby before walking to a wall plaque to figure out where he needed to go. Hearing a gurgle, he looked down at the infant he carried in front of him in a maroon sling. She looked up at him and he smiled. Sandy had called to say that her baby, Rachel Ann, seemed a little sick and might be getting her first tooth. Rather than send her to daycare, he said he would take her for the day. He put her pacifier back in her mouth and she pulled it out. Smiling at Rachel, he took the escalator to the fifth floor to the Western History and Genealogy Center.

"O'Malley!" A man's voice came from the office behind the counter.

"Les," Seth said.

"Jeez, man, I heard you were dating some sweet young thing, but don't you think that's a little young?" the voice said.

Seth laughed.

"Just a second," Les said.

When he heard a woman say, "I am not speaking to that man," he turned his back to the office to look out at the Western History and Genealogy Center. He had called before coming down. The head librarian had made sure Jocelyn was here when he arrived. That was all he would guarantee. Les and Jocelyn argued back and forth in a low, unintelligible rumble.

Seth took Rachel out of the sling. Rachel had wide blue eyes, light blonde curls, and her grandmother's big smile. Like her grandmother, Rachel's delicate beauty covered the heart of a lion.

He looked up when an elderly woman stormed out of the reference librarian's office. Her stiff walk was as tight as the bun on her head and support stockings. Rachel tugged on his hair. She laughed when he looked back at her.

The woman stopped in place.

Happy to have his full attention, Rachel showed him the new trick she'd learned from her elder brothers and sisters. She clapped. Before she could stop herself, the woman drifted over to them.

"She looks just like Andy," the woman whispered.

Knowing better than to say anything, Seth nodded. The woman sniffed.

"Did Andy get a chance . . .?"

"They met once, when she and Sandy met," Seth said. "Just a few hours before she died."

"I know I don't have a right, but . . ." The woman looked up at Seth and held her arms out. "May I?"

He smiled and set Rachel in her hands. Rachel clapped.

"She just learned to clap," Seth said. "She's pretty happy about it."

"That's very good," the woman said.

"This is Rachel Ann," Seth said.

"Nice to meet you, Rachel Ann."

Rachel put her hand on the woman's cheek as if she wanted her to say her name.

"I'm Jocelyn," the woman said.

Rachel looked at Seth as if he was to facilitate the introduction. Out of the corner of his eye, he saw the head librarian peek out of his office.

"Jocelyn is the Colorado historical librarian," Seth said to Rachel. "She knows everything about anything that happened in the state. She was a good friend of your grandmother, Andy Mendy, and . . ."

He leaned forward as if he was telling Rachel a secret.

"She doesn't like me much."

Rachel looked surprised and looked at Jocelyn. The librarian gave a tear-filled laugh.

"Did you bring her to soften me up?" Jocelyn asked.

"Sandy thinks her first tooth is coming in," Seth said. "She asked if I would keep an eye on her. Rachel and I are old friends. She came two months early. We had a hard fight to keep her with us."

Jocelyn's eyes scanned Seth's face. She nodded as if she understood.

"Why are you here?" Jocelyn asked.

"I wanted to look at the tax records from 1913," Seth said.

"Death of the tax agent?" Jocelyn asked.

"How'd you guess?" Seth asked.

"The CBI looked into it a few years ago," Jocelyn said. "Why are you interested?"

"I'm following up on a case for an old friend," Seth said. "Might be a link to the tax agent's death."

Jocelyn's mistrustful eyes watched him as if he was a deadly snake.

"You know, Sandy has all of Andy's belongings," Seth said. "It's taken a while, with the baby and everything, but I think she has a few things for you. We weren't sure . . .?"

"Like what?"

"Old photos, mostly," Seth said. "A few concert photos; there's a cute one of you and Andy performing outside . . ."

"Probably The Pops," Jocelyn smiled. "We played coast to coast in '69 and '70. You were redoing high school."

Seth smiled. Rachel made a loud "Bah!" and Jocelyn looked back at her.

"She likes to talk," Seth said. "Sandy has her husband's kids and her teenage brother and sister. Rachel's used to lots of chatting."

Jocelyn smiled at Rachel and then squinted at Seth.

"The death of the tax agent is one of my favorite stories," Jocelyn said. "Did you know that?"

"Not until Les told me."

"What do you want to know?"

"Anything you know," Seth said. "Never know what might lead us to the killer."

"You think the person who killed this guy is still killing people?" Jocelyn asked.

"Yes, Jocelyn, I think the same person is killing people across the country," Seth smiled.

"Zombies?"

"Vampire probably."

"I thought zombies were the thing now."

Seth smiled.

"How many people?"

"I know of sixty," Seth said. "I'm guessing maybe four hundred over the last hundred years or so."

"Four hundred people." Jocelyn's voice went low with disbelief.

Seth smiled. She watched him for a moment before seeming to come to some decision.

"I'll only help if you agree to one thing," Jocelyn said.

"What's that?"

"You have to come in and tell your personal story, warts and all, on record – audio, video and what not – for the library," Jocelyn said. "You're a living legend, Seth."

"Done."

"Oh, and you have to tell me what happens,"

Jocelyn said. "I always hate not knowing."

"I'll take you to lunch," Seth said.

"With Sandy and the baby?"

"I'll ask her," Seth said. "She only met Andy the one time. She hasn't met any of her mother's old friends. The whole thing is a little . . . confusing. I bet she'd like to meet you."

"Good. Follow me."

Jocelyn picked up Rachel, tucked her on her hip, and took off across the library floor. Seth had to hustle to keep up. Jocelyn pointed to a large, heavy book of maps.

"That one," Jocelyn said.

Seth picked it up and they trotted over to a small study room. Seth set the book on the table with a thud. Jocelyn stood by a chair until Seth realized she wanted him to pull it out for her. He did. She sat down with Rachel.

"Take a seat," Jocelyn said. "Did you bring a recorder?"

"Don't need one," Seth said. "I'll remember."

"You'll remember?" Her voice wasn't unkind, but relayed her disbelief.

"I remember everything, Jocelyn," Seth said.

"Everything?" Jocelyn eyes' flashed with compassion.

Seth pursed his lips and nodded.

"I'm sorry."

"That's why I drank so much," Seth said. "To forget."

"Did it work?"

"Not really," Seth said.

Jocelyn put her hand over his and gave it a squeeze. He nodded.

“Shall we?” Jocelyn asked.

“Please.”

EIGHT

"What do you know about property taxes?"

"Nothing," Seth said. "I think my mortgage pays them via escrow. I don't know; Sandy set it up. Should I call her?"

Jocelyn smiled.

"I'm a drug addict and alcoholic," Seth said. "Money and I don't mix."

She chuckled, and he shrugged.

"I meant the property tax system."

"Nothing," Seth said.

"I'll keep it relevant," Jocelyn smiled at Rachel. "Ulysses S. Grant declared Colorado a state in 1876. Property taxes were instituted that year."

"So fast?"

"Yes," Jocelyn said. "They looked around to see who could fund the new state and build all these nice buildings, and realized the railroad had to come through the state. The first property taxes were on the railroad and big business. The original tax board was created in 1876 and in 1877 a court ruling gutted the power from the board."

She looked up from Rachel to see if Seth was listening. He gave her an affirming nod.

"Anyway, there was a lot of this and that – create a board, disband a board, and on and on. Typical Colorado," she said. "In 1913, the State Tax Commission was created. This second board brought property taxes to regular people. 1913 was the first time residents and landowners – individuals – were taxed and the first time anyone had assessed the value of Colorado property."

"How much was Colorado worth?"

"I don't remember everything," Jocelyn smiled.

He smiled in return.

"Have you heard of the Great Blizzard of 1913?" Jocelyn asked.

"Maybe," Seth shrugged.

"Forty-five point seven inches dropped between December 1 and 6. It's the greatest amount of snowfall from one storm," she said. "The storm blanketed the western part of the state with snow. Georgetown was the hardest hit, with more than seven feet of snow. They say there were twenty-foot drifts."

"That's a lot of snow."

"More than twenty million tons of snow," she

nodded. "Transportation completely stopped; buildings collapsed under the weight of the snow; people and livestock died. They didn't have snow-moving equipment. They had to dig their way out with shovels and strong backs.

"Do you have one of those fancy phones?" she asked.

He shook his head.

"Well, you can look up the photos online," Jocelyn said. "They lined up the wagons and shoveled snow into them."

"And the tax agent?" Seth asked. Rachel said, "Bah!" and waved her fist.

"Yes, 'Get to the point Ms. Jocelyn,' Rachel says," Jocelyn chuckled at the baby. "Your grandmother used to say, 'Oh Jocelyn can go on and on.'"

Seth smiled.

"The tax agent set out from Denver on the first of November. His goal was to work his way through the larger ranches and end up in Trinidad by Thanksgiving. His family met him at the Columbia Hotel downtown."

Seth had the sense that these little details were important. He leaned back to take it all in.

"His name was Paul Bradley. He was the younger brother of Peter Bradley. Heard of him?"

Seth shook his head.

"Peter Bradley was an industrialist who specialized in fertilizer, lumber, and heavy machinery. He was the silent partner in importing and breeding Arabian horses in the US. Lived in Boston," Jocelyn said. "He sent his brother out to Colorado to buy timber and grazing land, get in good with the mining operations to sell machinery, and see what else he could invest in. That's officially why he sent his brother."

"His letters indicate that he actually sent his brother to Colorado to create a pipeline for his horses. Paul Bradley took the tax agent job as a way of getting to know ranchers all over the state. As you can imagine, no one was all that happy about having foreign horses here in Colorado."

"As a tax man, he would be out on the ranches," Seth said. "He'd know what ranches were ready to fold, where the virgin timber was . . ."

"And which ranchers were willing to raise Arabian horses."

"That's smart."

"Brilliant," Jocelyn said. "On this trip, he bought a couple of ranches outside of Walsenburg before meeting his family for Thanksgiving. His family took the train and lingered until the first of December. His wife's letters indicate that she sent him off in his buggy around the first of December."

"At the start of the blizzard," Seth said.

"There wasn't a national weather forecast then," Jocelyn said. "Like a lot of Colorado snowstorms, the blizzard started with just a little snow. Paul Bradley was from back East. He wouldn't have known how things can change on a dime here. He set out from Trinidad. His records, the ones they found on him, indicate that he made slow progress up the valley. The last notation is the fourth of December 1913, the day eyewitnesses say all hell broke loose. When they found Mr. Bradley, they assumed his buggy had gotten stuck and he had frozen to death out there."

"When did they find him?"

"About two months after he disappeared," she said. "It wasn't until he thawed out that they saw the bullet hole."

"Where did they find him?" Seth asked.

She opened the heavy map book and began flipping the pages.

"There."

Jocelyn pointed to a small town off a railway line that ran up the center of the valley. Seth pulled his reading glasses from the breast pocket of his sports jacket and leaned over to look.

"In between Tyrone and Thatcher?" he asked.

"It's called Houghton, now," she said. "All of these railway towns were named after valley cattlemen – owners of the big ranches. Thatcher, Model, Louden, Tyrone, Bloom . . . Most of these families homesteaded this land in the late 1880s and early 1900s."

"Why do those names and this land sound familiar?"

"The U.S. Army has a large training facility there."

"Piñon Canyon."

"They bought and took the land in the 1980s," Jocelyn said. "Opened the maneuver site in 1983."

"Tried a land grab some years back?"

"The Army?" Jocelyn nodded. "It's these people,

the Loudens, Thatchers, Tyrones, and Blooms – people who've lived in the area for a long time – they've fought the Army for years. Right now, they have a reprieve, but you know how this works. The Army is never going to give up; so the families keep fighting."

"These families still live there," Seth said.

"This flat, open valley will always be home to them. It doesn't look like much . . ."

"The Army says it looks like Iraq," Seth smiled.

"It's home for them," Jocelyn said. "Has been since before Colorado was a state."

"You think they killed the tax agent?" Seth asked.

"No one knows," Jocelyn said. "The sheriff at the time thought he probably killed himself."

"He knew he was stranded, saw the storm intensify, figured he couldn't get out," Seth said. "Suicide was better than freezing to death?"

"That's what they determined," Jocelyn said.

"Then why was it marked as an unsolved case?" Seth asked.

"If it was a suicide, the tax agent's family wouldn't get a death pay out," Jocelyn said. "Big expensive lawyer from Boston showed up and made a fuss. Mr. Bradley had a wife and a couple of young kids. The sheriff felt sorry for them."

"Huh," Seth said. "And the horses?"

"I knew you'd catch that," Jocelyn said. "No one knows what happened to his Arabian horses. That's part of the mystery. Was he killed for the horses? Was it a tax problem? I'll tell you though. There's lots of talk about the amazing horses from this valley. They're prized by endurance horse race fanatics. My daughter says if she doesn't place in the Pony Express Trail 100 this year, she's going to get a horse from Piñon Valley."

"Are they Arabian horses?"

"They don't look it," Jocelyn said. "But if I were still a guitar-swinging, rock 'n roll gal, I'd wager they're the descendents of Paul Bradley's horses."

Seth nodded. Rachel smacked her lips and started a chant of "Ma, Ma, Ma."

"I hate to get info and run, but that's the sound she makes before she starts . . ."

Rachel let out a wail.

"Crying," Seth said. "She's hungry."

"Did you bring . . ."

Seth scowled at Jocelyn. Their long-held disdain for each other reappeared. He dug around in the bag Sandy had given him to find a bottle of breast milk. He was about to take Rachel from her when Jocelyn yanked the bottle away. She checked the temperature. She gave him a kind of "so there" look and began feeding Rachel.

"I heard you're getting married again," Jocelyn looked up at him. "Does she know about Andy?"

"She does."

"And she's okay with that?"

"She says that knowing I love and loved someone so deeply means that I'm able to love. Being able to love is a rare gift," Seth said. Jocelyn looked surprised. He lifted a shoulder. "She's twenty-three."

"Young people are so much more emotionally

aware than we were," Jocelyn said. Seth nodded.

"She's Aaron Alvin's daughter," Seth said.

"Poor girl," Jocelyn said. "That man is a bastard. How are they doing?"

"Not great," Seth said.

"She's lucky to have you." When Jocelyn looked up, her eyes were filled with tears. "Andy was too. I know that, it's just that . . ."

"It's easier to hate me than believe we couldn't work it out."

She gave a slight nod.

"It's easier for me too," he smiled.

She nodded and looked down at Rachel.

"I think she's asleep," Jocelyn said.

"She sleeps for a little bit after she eats," he got up from his seat. "Then it's burping, diapers, and play. I'd better get her home, or I'll never hear the end of it from her teenage playmates."

Jocelyn set Rachel in his arms. Rachel fussed for a moment, and then fell back to sleep. Seth settled the baby in her sling. He picked up the book of maps and they walked into the open library space.

"The CBI thought there might be some connection between the tax agent and the Civil War – Confederate Army specifically," Seth said.

Jocelyn shrugged.

"Anything?"

"In that area? Sure," Jocelyn said. "Why don't I take a look? I'll let you know if I can pin down anything specific."

"Thanks," Seth said.

Jocelyn looked as if she was going to say something. Instead, she turned in place and walked back across the library. Seth watched her go, then set the map book back on its shelf. Rachel stirred and he took her into the bathroom to change her diaper. She smiled at him and fell sound asleep.

|-||-|||-||-|||-||-|||-||-|||-||-|||-||-|||-||-|||

Nine

Somewhere between dropping Rachel off in Uptown and his house in Park Hill, the passageway to where music lived clicked open. As it had since that day in second grade, music flooded in. The rhythm pounded in his brain. The sound filled his ears. His nose filled with the sweet smell of melody. He had to lean forward to focus on driving. He made it to his driveway before his sight filled. Before his eyes, he saw dancing black notes on a white page.

Seth stumbled from his car and fumbled with the lock on the garden gate. He was about to call the house when the gate opened. Ava stood in front of him. Under music's spell, he had the overwhelming desire to make love to her right there. She smiled with the memory of the times they had done just that. They both looked in the direction of the sound of her mother's laugh.

He was infused with music, not insane. There was no way he was going to get caught making love on the lawn by her mother. Ava leaned forward to acknowledge his thoughts.

Taking his hand, she helped him through the gate. She slipped down the backstairs to avoid their house guests. She took his key from his hand and helped him into his piano sanctuary. When he turned, Ava kissed him with hard promise and touched her hand to his heart. He smiled. With a nod, she closed the door.

He sat down at the piano and felt the music well. His last conscious thought was to turn on the digital recorder.

The music took him away.

He played until his fingers hurt. He played until he had to fight to keep his eyes open. Closing his heavy lids, he played until the music slipped away.

He stumbled from the bench to the bathroom. When he returned, he noticed Ava curled up on the leather couch. Wrapped in his mother's quilts, she had been there for hours. He lay down on the rug in front of her and fell sound asleep.

When he woke a couple of hours later, he knew two things – that the music he'd created last night was good, and that all of this killing was connected in some way to property taxes in southeastern Colorado. Once he'd polished and finished the music, his agent would package and sell it.

It was up to him to find the killers. With murder-for-hire, he knew where to start.

Like always, his music surge left him awake and invigorated. He touched Ava's sleeping face. She opened her eyes and smiled.

"Are you back?" she asked.

"For you," he said.

She joined him on the floor.

|-||-|||-||-|||-||-|||-||-|||-||-|||-||-|||-||-|||

Ten

Seth leaned back in his office chair to look at the map of the U.S. he'd tacked on the wall. He'd placed a yellow self-sticking flag over every city with a cluster of three or four unsolved killings over the course of a summer. The map was covered with yellow. Hearing a sound behind him, Seth rotated his office chair around to find Ava's sister Éowyn standing in the doorway.

"So, that's what you do here?" Éowyn spoke in her usual sneering tone. Seth heard Éowyn's desperate unhappiness echo between her words. He smiled.

"What is?" He rotated his chair back around to look at the large map. He gestured to a chair near him. She slunk into the room.

"Music, mystery, sex," Éowyn said as she dropped

into the seat.

"I was supposed to be on vacation," Seth said.

"Seems like a vacation," she said.

"Don't tell anyone," Seth rotated to look at her.

"Why?"

"People pay me a lot of money to do this, and I don't want them to know," Seth said.

Éowyn's lip lifted into a kind of sideways smile. The rest of her face held her sorrow and exhaustion. She seemed to be searching for something to say.

"You make a lot of money as a cop?" Éowyn asked.

"Sex," Seth laughed.

She gave him the gift of a genuine smile.

"What are you working on?" Éowyn asked.

"Little mystery brought to me by an old friend," Seth said.

She went to the wall to look at the map.

"And the flags?"

"Cities with murders that fit the profile," Seth said.

"That's a lot of murder," Éowyn said. "One city per state?"

"Looks that way," Seth said. "It's hard to tell because the records only go back so far."

"This has been going on a long time?"

"I think so," Seth said. "Ava thinks so. That's part of the mystery."

"And the FBI?"

"No standard protocol; no standard weapon . . ."

"No M.O.," Éowyn nodded. "That *is* a good mystery. Serial killer?"

"Murder-for-hire," Seth shrugged. "I think. Mostly it's a lot of unsolved murders that span the country and go on for a lot of years. Or . . ."

Seth's eyes shifted to the map.

"Or?"

"Or there's a bunch of detectives who like Maresol's cooking enough to massage their unsolved cases to fit this project," Seth said.

"We know that's true," Éowyn said. "What's your next move?"

"I have a call in to someone I knew in the Army," Seth said. "We'll see what he knows about murder-for-hire. Otherwise, I don't have a clue who is behind this. I'm still collecting murders."

"How many people were killed a year?"

"Four," Seth said. "Sometimes three. In the fifties, it was only two or three. But it's been four for a while."

"Odd how no one noticed all these years," she said.

"It's hard to imagine," Seth said. "But computers are pretty new. These murders went on for at least seventy years before cops had access to computers and another twenty before they were common."

Seth's eyes shifted to look at Éowyn. Thin and technically beautiful, Ava's elder sister had an exacting nature that came through in her perfectly arched eyebrows, her manicured fingertips, and her stern social grace. This morning, all of that perfection made her look lost and very alone.

"How are you?" he asked.

"Wondering what I want to know." Her eyes flitted

over his face. He nodded. "What I wanted to see, with my Dad, you know?"

He waited for her to add more to her thoughts. When she didn't, he turned back to look at the map.

"Want to play mystery?" Seth asked.

"I'm not going to play sex," Éowyn said the words as if they were daggers.

"You know, you can talk to me," Seth said. "I might actually be one of the few people who understand."

"Oh yeah?" Her lip made an effort to sneer. If she hadn't been so exhausted she would have seemed cruel. But today, she seemed lost. "What do you understand?"

"I know what it's like to do what you're supposed to, be what you're supposed to be, and feel like you're missing something because you're so miserable," Seth said.

Éowyn became still. As if she was ready to strike, her eyes watched him with exacting intensity.

"I don't know why I knew how to play the piano," Seth said. "It was like having blue eyes or black hair . . ."

"Or having an analytical mind," she said.

"I was ten when I was shipped off to Eastman," Seth said.

"I was twelve when I won my first national debate tournament," she said.

"You see?" Seth smiled. "We have a lot in common."

She nodded.

"Can I ask you a question?" she asked.

"Of course."

"Do you love it?" she asked.

"Piano?" Seth's eyebrows went up with the question and she nodded. "It's more than love, obsession maybe, but . . ."

Embarrassed, he looked away from her.

"But?"

"Oh, nothing," he said. "I was going to say that I don't love the press of composition or the moment the music comes. It's like an overpowering urge for sex – an almost physical pain that requires a kind of desperate release. But the truth of the matter is that I feel so alive when the music comes. It's as if every fiber, every tissue, every cell in my body vibrates with passion. It's a rush that . . . well, I guess is . . . hard to explain.

"I'm miserable if I only play the piano. I can retreat from the world in my basement and play for days at a time. Once I've been down there for a week or so, I start to think of drugs and alcohol and . . . Well, let's just say it doesn't suit me."

"That's why you're a cop?" Éowyn asked.

"Music and mysteries go hand in hand," Seth said. "My agent says my music is better when I'm working on a case. I think the mysteries occupy my thinking mind and get me out of the house. That leaves the rest of me open and receptive to music. I solve puzzles while I'm composing. In the last ten years or so, I've written a new piece for every big case."

"This is a big case then."

"I guess so," Seth said. "Can I ask you a question?"

She nodded.

"What do you love to do?" he asked.

As if she'd never heard the question before, her mouth fell open. She gave a slight shake of her head and scowled.

"Not being a lawyer," he said.

"How . . .?"

"We've tried two cases together?"

"Three," she said.

"If you watch the DA in court, he loves being there. He struts around like a peacock in heat," Seth said. "I've had lunch with him where he repeats every glorious word from his day in court. He loves everything about being in court. He even loves the politics. But you . . .?"

"If you're saying I'm not any good at being a DA, you're wrong," she said. "I have the best record of any deputy DA in the state. No one else is even close."

"I asked you what you love to do." Seth's tone was even and kind, but she reacted as if she'd been hit. She jumped from her seat and raised her index finger like a dagger.

"I'll tell you that I graduated Phi Beta Kappa at CU Boulder and was first in my class at Stanford," she said. "I didn't need my father's help getting my job. Prosecutor's offices lined up to get a chance for me to work with them. I don't expect to have any trouble replacing my job. None."

"And?"

As if he'd pulled a string attached to her belly button, she collapsed into the chair. She covered her face with her hands and cried. To give her some privacy, he waded through his email. There was lots of chatter about his case, but no new facts.

Who was behind all of this murder? He'd almost forgotten Éowyn was there when she gave a kind of cough or a laugh. He rotated his chair to look at her.

"Knitting." Her voice was light and her face lit up in a smile. "I love to knit."

He was so surprised by her words that he couldn't think of anything to say. She gave a sad shrug.

"Can't make a living knitting things," she said.

"What about owning a store?"

She blinked at him for a few moments before she looked away.

"A knitting store," Seth said. "A yarn store. Something high-end to suit your . . ."

"My snotty ways?" she smirked. He smiled. "How am I going to launch my own store when I'm flat broke?"

"How does anyone?" he asked.

"That's what I'm asking."

"I have no idea," he said.

"Oh."

He watched her closely as the silence dragged into almost a minute. When she said, "Who would?" he smiled.

"My agent, James Schmidt, Jr., has a step-mother who owns a little fashion shop," Seth said.

"Which one?"

"Annabel's."

"Nice," Éowyn said.

"I bet she'd tell us everything we want to know," Seth said.

"We?"

"Why not?" Seth asked. "Unless you weren't

serious."

"No, I'm serious," she said. "I've wanted to do this very thing – own my own knitting store – for . . . well, since my grandmother taught me to knit when I was thirteen."

"My family has a homestead outside of Granby," Seth said. "A lot of people have alpaca and sheep in that valley. You could always go 'Made in Colorado' and stock only wool from here."

"I hadn't thought of it," she smiled. Lost in thought, Ava's sister fell silent. She looked down and then at Seth. "What about being a lawyer?"

"What about it?" Seth asked. "You can always volunteer if you want to keep your hand in. Do you know my agent, James Schmidt? He goes by Jammy or Schmidty? He's about your age. Took over from his dad about three years ago."

"I don't think so."

"He graduated top of his law school class, yada, yada. I bet he'll be all over this."

"You mean take over it?"

"No," Seth said. "If you're going to do this, it has to be your baby."

She nodded.

"It's a lot to take in," he said. "Why don't you think about it?"

"I've thought about it almost all my life," she said. "Will you call your agent?"

Seth picked up his phone and made the call. His young agent's excited voice drifted through the phone. When Seth hung up, he turned to look at Éowyn.

"Sorry about that," Seth said. "He's dating my daughter, Lizzy, and wanted to know if he could marry her."

"Congratulations," Éowyn said.

"It's not a huge surprise. He's been in love with her since they were little," Seth said. "She's had a few . . . issues."

"You suck as a dad?"

"I'm sure I do, but these particular issues have more to due with her mother and step-father. Anyway, he'll call me when he's spoken with his step-mother."

"Great," she said. "What's next?"

"I'd encourage you to rest," Seth said. "You've been through a horrible ordeal, and retail is no picnic."

Getting up from her seat, she nodded to him. She was almost to the door when she turned around.

"You know, most of your murders are along major highways," Éowyn said. "I bet your guy drove there."

"Sure."

"If I were you, I'd check parking tickets; speeding tickets; stuff like that," she said.

"You think he's that stupid?"

"Look at your time frame," she said. "That's a lot of cities. He's traveling to cities he doesn't live in. Over the course of all these years? No one's that good. Just random chance says he's had a ticket or two. And even if the tickets are ten years apart in different cars, you might come up with his name. Who knows? They may even have a picture of him on some traffic cam."

"Good idea," Seth said. "Thanks."

"Analytical mind," she said, and left the room.

Seth thought for a moment and began making calls.

|-||-|||-||-|||-||-|||-||-|||-||-|||-||-|||-||-|||

Eleven

Seth navigated the double gates and stepped into the fenced area of the dog park before letting Clara off her leash. She rubbed her head against his leg for a moment and he rubbed her ears. When the moment of bonding passed, she zoomed off to meet the other dogs. She gave an excited bark and playful bow to Zephyr, the Rhodesian Ridgeback. Zephyr mimicked her bow, and they began romping around on the flat dirt. Seth moved toward a quiet end of the dog park and waited.

"I forget that my Anjelika takes the majestic Zephyr to play with your puppy," a man said as he walked toward Seth.

His deep, rich voice had the lilt of British Africa. At least a decade older than Seth, he carried himself in a way that spoke of physical prowess. Seth had never heard his given name; he went by the name Perses. Someone had told Mitch that Perses had barely survived the meltdown of Rhodesia. His sisters were raped and murdered before his eyes. Perses vowed to avenge their deaths. Over the course of the next ten years, he'd done just that.

Hired by a special branch of the CIA during the Cold War, Perses was credited with "solving problems" around the globe. When he wasn't working, Perses lived in Denver with his Anjelika, a former Russian-Mob princess. Their adult children, and grandchildren, lived nearby. Seth knew him to have two weaknesses – his family and chocolate.

Seth held out a travel mug to Perses. The man's eyebrows furrowed for a moment before he took the cup. He unscrewed the cap and gave a little cheer for the Mexican hot chocolate in the cup.

"Maresol loves me," Perses took a sip.

"She does," Seth said.

"Don't tell my Angel," Perses said. "She might get jealous."

Seth chuckled. They stood in the cool, early morning and watched the dogs play.

"I found something of yours." Seth said. He took a small evidence bag from the interior pocket of his jacket. "I believe you left this in your son-in-law's skull."

Seth held the small zipper storage bag up in front of Perses eyes.

"Has your mark," Seth pointed to the Greek letters etched on the bullet.

"What does it have to do with me?" Perses shrugged.

Seth raised an eyebrow and said nothing.

"He divorced my Jillian," Perses said. "No connection to me."

Seth held up the bag.

"What do you want, O'Malley?" Perses's demeanor tightened. The air seemed to crackle with tension. For the briefest moment, the civility disappeared and the improbable stories about the man seemed all too true.

"Information," Seth said.

"About this bullet?"

"What's to know about this?" Seth asked. "You shot your ex-son-in-law while he was in the act of committing a class one felony. You were due a freebie, so the Agency fixed it via a Special Forces team. Ex-son-in-laws wife is in prison for life on a separate crime committed at the same time. His parents tried to kidnap a senator's son. They're out of the way."

Seth shrugged.

"And the case?"

"Dismantled," Seth said. "All but this."

Seth held up the bullet.

"You've been saving it for a favor?" Perses asked.

"No, I don't believe I need to bribe you for favors," Seth said. "I've been waiting for a right moment to return your property. With being sick, the wedding, Saint Jude . . ."

"You've had an interesting year," Perses said.

"Yes," Seth said. "I do need information. Clara

loves her buddy Zephyr. It seemed like a good time to . . ."

"Kill a few birds," Perses smiled.

With that, his charming demeanor returned like the sun on a stormy day. Seth returned his smile. Perses took the zipper storage bag and tucked it into his jacket. Clara gave a loud bark, and they watched the dogs play for a few minutes.

"Are you heading out again?" Seth asked.

"Me?" Perses asked. "No. They prefer to use drones to solve problems now. Less likely to give up information in some foreign prison. I am . . . retired. It's different; nice. You should try it."

Seth nodded.

"How's the music?" Perses asked.

"Good," Seth said. "I'm working on a new piece."

"You must have a case," Perses said.

"Killer-for-hire," Seth said. "You remember McGinty?"

Perses nodded.

"He has sarcoidosis," Seth said.

"Agent Orange. Like Mitch."

"Not according to the V.A., but yeah," Seth said. "This is his case."

Seth took a drink of his coffee and waited for Perses. He knew if he moved too fast, the man would clam up. He had to take his time.

"McGinty found five cities with four or so killings a year in the nineties," Seth said. "I found four or so killings in every medium-to-small city in the country."

"Except Colorado."

"One outside of Trinidad in 1913," Seth said. "Tax agent."

Perses's left eyebrow lifted, but his face remained still. The assassin's eyes noticed that the dogs had stopped playing. He took a ball from his pocket, whistled for Zephyr, and threw the ball. The dogs took off after the ball and Perses turned to look at Seth.

"He's not one of us," Perses said.

"He?"

"Bunch of *he's*," Perses said. "His grandfather, father, and himself. We have a file."

"Why?" Seth asked.

"Why do you think?"

"You've been watching him kill U.S. Citizens for almost a hundred years," Seth said.

"That's dark," Perses said. "And unlikely. If you're interested, I can see if I can get it redacted."

"Highlights?"

Perses fell silent again. He threw the ball for the dogs a few times before he turned back to Seth.

"Sure," Perses said. "I can't think of a reason why not. The entire family is a pestilence. There was a time when people like me served a global purpose. My team was created after World War II. We've saved lives, prevented wars and . . . Anyway, it's not a purpose my son Stephen will ever agree with but it is a reason other than money to pay taxes – his property taxes, no less."

"He kills for the money to pay his property taxes?" Seth asked.

"That's the irony," Perses said. "He says the tax man

– the one from 1913 – said, 'I don't care what you do to get the money. You live on this land; you have to pay these taxes.' His great-grandfather was in the business for the Confederacy; good at it too."

"To pay their taxes?" Seth shook his head.

"To pay their property taxes," Perses said.

"Four a summer," Seth said.

"They're school teachers who own a very large ranch," Perses said. "Plus, they have the summers off."

"How does he pick a city?" Seth asked.

"One he hasn't been to," Perses shrugged.

"Military brass?" Seth asked.

"You found some?" Perses asked.

"Five or six," Seth said. "Over the course of the last few decades."

"They own a shooting range on the way to Piñon Canyon," Perses said. "A lot of military stop there on their way out and back. Friendly competition; things like that."

"Tire lead?"

"Same way everyone gets it," Perses shrugged. "Local tire shops. There's a few in Trinidad you could call. I bet they know him."

"He teaches in Trinidad, Colorado?"

"Near there," Perses said.

Seth thought for a moment before saying, "Hoehne High School?"

Perses rewarded him with, "Science teacher."

"He's up for elimination?" Seth asked.

Perses confirmed his statement with a raise of one eyebrow. Seth weighed the idea in his mind. If he let the case linger, more people would die, and so would his killer. He took a long drink of his coffee before acknowledging to himself that he'd never be satisfied with that outcome.

"You?" Seth asked.

"I'm retired."

"Drone?"

"You're asking the wrong question," Perses took a drink of his hot chocolate. "I do love Maresol."

"I'll make sure she knows," Seth said.

The men fell silent. Seth could feel the seconds ticking away. Soon, Perses would whistle for Zephyr, and he would have lost the goodwill brought on by the return of the bullet.

"Looks like the Army is going through with the expansion of Piñon Canyon," Perses said.

"I thought that was off," Seth said. "A done deal."

"Not according to the ranchers there," Perses said. "A few of them have already sold their land to the Army and are getting out. Off of the land; out of the business."

"And our high school science teacher?" Seth asked.

"Had girls," Perses said. "You have daughters. You know how they are. They're interested in horses, beauty pageants, and marrying doctors. They aren't up for the business of murder – not mine, not yours, and not his. This is his last season."

"And the last contract?"

Perses gave Seth a beaming smile. That must have been the right question.

"Politician," Perses said. "I never met the man, but I hear he's a miscreant."

As if Seth should know who he was referring to, Perses glanced at him. Seth gave a slight shrug.

"Contract includes his wife and children," Perses said. "Our killer-for-hire took a large contract for his last. Money for taxes. Money to relocate. And it has a heavy purse. Looks like a lot of people wanted this guy gone."

"You?"

"Not us."

Seth felt like he was missing something. Racking his brain, he looked away for a moment.

"Who bought the services?" Seth asked the lazy cop's question.

Perses shook his head. That wasn't the question Seth was supposed to ask.

"Where is he relocating?" Seth asked.

Perses shook his head. As if he was trying to send Seth the information, the assassin's eyes burrowed into Seth's very soul. He asked the only question he could think of. Who was this assassin?

"Who?" Seth asked.

"Alvin," Perses said.

Seth gaped at the man. Perses nodded.

"All five plus a few others," Perses took a drink of hot chocolate. Over the brim of the mug, he said in a low tone, "Did you know Aaron Alvin is here right now?"

"I . . ." Seth pointed to the gate.

Perses whistled for Zephyr. Seth grabbed Clara as she ran by and took off toward the parking lot. Clara jumped into his sedan. He was dialing the phone as he sat down in the passenger seat.

"Answer. Answer. Answer," he repeated as Ava's phone rang.

Twelve

"Seth! You heard!" Ava yelled over the familiar scream of a police siren.

"I heard?"

"It's Bella," Ava said. "She's been shot. Captain Ferguson called. That's all I know."

"Where are you?" Seth asked.

"Denver Health," Ava said. "Cruiser escort. We just pulled in. Are you coming?"

"I'll be there," Seth closed his eyes to say a silent prayer of gratitude. He was about to hang up when he heard the sharp report of a handgun.

"Ah crap," Ava said, and the line went dead.

Seth drove like a mad man through the streets of Denver. He desperately missed his Denver Police badge and bubble siren. Finally at the Denver Health parking lot, he had to wait until a parking space cleared before he could park.

"I have to go in," he said to Clara.

She seemed to know exactly what was going on. He rolled the window down on her side. He ruffled her head and ran across the parking lot. He arrived at the entrance to emergency to find Ava's mother and her older sister near the door. They were holding each other and weeping. Ava was standing near the desk filling out paperwork and talking to a uniformed police officer. Moving toward Ava, he noticed two U.S. marshals striding across the waiting room toward him.

"O'Malley," the first marshal said. His booming voice caused Ava to spin in place. She ran to him. Her entire body trembled in his arms. She held him tight and pressed her face into the crook of his neck. He shifted her to his left side and looked up when the marshal approached.

"Jasper," Seth said.

"What do you know?" Deputy U.S. Marshal Jasper asked.

"Nothing," Seth said. "Was someone shot in the parking lot?"

"Fireworks," Deputy U.S. Marshal Jasper nodded. "I thought it was shots too."

"Celebrating a baby," Deputy U.S. Marshal Jasper's partner, Deputy U.S. Marshal Kowalski said. "You here to celebrate a baby?"

Seth's eyes flicked to Ava.

"Your daughter?" Jasper asked.

"Fiancé," Seth said.

Jasper gave him an assessing look. Seth scowled at him.

"She's one of Alvin's girls," Kowalski said.

"Amelie?" Seth shifted Ava from him.

Her tear-stained face looked up at him. He gave her a soft smile. They both knew he would get more information without her there.

"I need to finish paying for . . . for . . ." She pointed to the desk where she'd been, and he nodded. She wrapped her arms around herself and went back to filling out the paperwork.

"Why are you here?" Seth asked.

"Alvin," Jasper said. "He was one of ours."

"Was?"

Jasper and Kowalski nodded.

"What happened?" Seth asked.

"He was having brunch with his youngest daughter," Kowalski said.

"He wanted to see that woman . . ." Jasper said.

"Yvonne Smith?" Seth asked.

"Yeah, that woman he's obsessed with," Jasper said.

"You mean the woman he forced into prostitution and held captive for more than twenty years with threats to her wrongfully incarcerated husband," Seth raised his eyebrows at Jasper. "That's not to mention what he did to her daughter."

"Yeah, her," Jasper cleared his throat and looked away.

"She's out of town," Kowalski said. "Trip to the

coast, care of the U.S. Marshal Service."

"He settled for seeing his youngest daughter," Jasper said. "The girl begged the office."

"I thought . . ."

"Right," Kowalski said. "He's supposed to have zero contact with his family. Zero. We'd never heard of anything like it."

"You have it in writing?" Seth asked.

"You better f. . . uh . . ." Kowalski looked around the room. "Yes, O'Malley, we have it."

"Someone screwed up," Jasper said.

"Or was well paid," Seth said.

"What?" Kowalski shook his head at Seth.

"You first," Seth said. "What happened?"

"Stashed him at the Hyatt downtown," Jasper said. "He was due to testify this afternoon. The daughter came this morning, and we ordered room service. They were together . . ." Jasper looked at Kowalski.

"Ten minutes," Kowalski shrugged.

"Ten minutes," Jasper leaned close to Seth. "She gets there, they hug, we check the room, go over the rules, and step outside."

"Their food hadn't even arrived when . . ."

"Through the window from the office building across from the Hyatt," Jasper's voice was so low Seth wasn't sure he heard it.

Seth gave a slight shake of his head.

"High-powered rifle; armor-piercing bullet," Kowalski held two fingers to his heart. "Double. Straight through the heart."

"Both of them," Jasper said. "Bap, bap, . . . bap, bap. The curtains were closed."

"They were falling when we got the door open," Kowalski's voice dropped an octave. "We . . ."

"CPR – whole nine," Jasper said.

"It was a hit," Seth said.

"Or something," Kowalski said.

"I'm telling you it was a hit," Seth said. "When this happened, I was with someone who knows."

The marshals turned their full attention to Seth.

"All of them," Seth said.

The marshals' faces flushed. They looked away from Seth.

"No brass?" Jasper asked.

"Tire weight lead," Seth said.

"Have to wait for the coroner," Jasper said.

"How?" Kowalski asked.

"A dying friend asked me to look into what he thought was a few cases in the nineties," Seth said. "Murder-for-hire; three to five hits a summer in medium-to-small cities across the country; first one in 1913. I'm closing in on a name."

"Your contact didn't know?" Jasper asked.

"Didn't say," Seth said. "And Bella?"

Seth's voice cracked, and he cleared his throat. Even though he hadn't known her long, he'd been very fond of the spunky girl. He looked away to control his sorrow.

"Got her heart going again, but they couldn't keep it going." Jasper shook his head.

"She didn't suffer," Kowalski said. "Neither did he,

the bastard. I . . ."

The U.S. marshals looked at each other. Jasper shook his head and Kowalski closed his mouth.

"Hate is not really a strong enough word when used for that man," Seth said.

The marshals nodded in agreement.

"What are you going to do?" Seth asked.

"Clean up," Jasper said. "We're relieved of duty, which means we have piles of paperwork."

"What are you going to do?" Kowalski asked.

"Catch the killer before he . . ." Seth nodded his head toward Ava.

"Good plan," Jasper said.

|-||-|||-||-|||-||-|||-||-|||-||-|||-||-|||-||-|||

THIRTEEN

"Jeb just called," Seth said as he entered his bedroom. "They've turned onto I-70. They'll be here soon."

Ava's mother, Vivian, was packing her suitcase with her new clothing. Ava and Éowyn sat on the bed.

"Amelie? Éowyn?" Vivian looked at her daughters. "I need a moment with Seth."

"But . . ." Éowyn started.

"Please," In the silent way of powerful women, Vivian lowered her head to look at the floor.

"Come on, E," Amelie said. "Let's make sure you're all packed."

"Thank you," Vivian said.

Vivian watched her daughters leave the room. She waited for the door to close, before turning to Seth.

"I know what you think of me," Vivian said.

"What's that?"

"You think I was the stupid wife," Vivian said. "I lived in the big house, drank the wine, went to the spa, and spent the money while Aaron was out . . ."

Seth watched her struggle for words. As if she was going to cry, her lip vibrated. Her eyes shot hot embers.

"I didn't know," Vivian said. "And . . . how could I not know?"

Seth took a step further into the room.

"I knew he was infatuated with Yvonne, you know, Yvonne Smith," Vivian nodded her head. "But I had no idea he . . . or the depth of which he . . . and . . . I'm not a stupid woman. Sure, he wasn't as attentive . . . to me, the girls . . . as he was when we were first married, but he was the Colorado Attorney General for God's sake. And . . . "

She looked up at him. He tracked the lines her despair had etched lines onto her face.

"Should I have known?" she asked.

"I don't think so."

"Did you know?"

"Yes."

"How?"

"Mitch and I had the perp in custody," Seth said. "He confessed to killing and raping the girl, the one Rodney Smith went to prison for. Your husband, he . . ."

Vivian nodded.

"I remember that time," Vivian said. "He was very agitated, excited almost, couldn't sleep, didn't eat, paced around. I was pregnant with . . . Amelie, I guess. My mother said to just ignore him. 'Men get like that when their wives are pregnant.'"

"And they're stealing another man's wife," Seth said.

"Yes, that's what he was doing," Vivian nodded. "Makes you wonder about Helen."

"Of Troy?" Seth's quick smile was lost to Vivian.

"Is she . . . ? I mean, is Yvonne . . .?"

"She's good," Seth said. "Happy."

"Does she hate me?"

"No. Yvonne feels horribly for you and the girls," Seth said. "Like the rest of us, she can't believe what he's done. She called him the spider. He really was . . . a terrible person."

"When I come back," Vivian's eyes scanned Seth's face. "Will you set up a meeting with her? For me? Maybe Éowyn, too?"

"I think she'd like that," Seth nodded. "She called Amelie when she heard that you would lose the house and . . . everything."

"She did?"

Seth nodded.

"Leave him alone," Vivian said. "That's what my mother said. 'He's an important man with important things on his mind. Focus on the girls, your house, and leave him alone.' But . . . now I look at it, and somewhere, in the middle of it all, I knew. I knew what he was up to. I did know."

"Of course you did," Seth said.

"And all of this," Vivian said. "Throwing me and

the girls to the sharks. Giving the Feds every penny we had, our home, our whole life, the life we built, I built . . . They took my wedding ring, my twentieth anniversary ring, and . . . He tossed us away. And now . . . my Bella."

Vivian broke down. Seth stepped to her. He opened his arms to offer her a shoulder to cry on. She held on and soundlessly weep.

"Did she suffer?" Vivian whispered.

"No."

"Did he?"

"No."

"That's too bad," Vivian stepped back. She thanked him with a nod and turned her back. He waited while she collected herself. She looked calm and steady when she turned around. "Sorry about that . . ."

"I've lost two children," Seth said. "There's nothing that describes the pain. And knowing that their other parent was responsible for their death, makes a horrible thing just that much more awful."

"Unbearable," Vivian nodded. "And if Éowyn or Amelie . . . I know she's been distant, and she insists on being called Ava and . . ."

"I think Jeb can keep you safe," Seth said. "But if he doesn't . . ."

"What do you mean?" Vivian asked.

Seth plastered on a smile. Her eyes asked the question again. He shook his head.

"Please," Vivian said. "I've lived with enough secrets to last a life time. Please just tell me the truth."

"We don't know who's behind all of this," Seth

said. “We may never know. Aaron betrayed everyone.”

“Why?” Vivian asked. “That’s what I don’t get. Why would he do this?”

Seth watched her for a moment.

“Oh my God,” Vivian said. “He traded it all for Yvonne.”

“And witness protection,” Seth said.

Vivian collapsed onto the bed and stared off into space.

“I know you need time to grieve,” Seth said. “I know you need space. But this is not the time.”

She looked up at him.

“Jeb Elliot,” Seth said. “Why was he here? He’s the sheriff. He was with his dying wife while these cases were investigated. He knows nothing about them. Did he say why he was here?”

Vivian gave a slight shake of her head.

“Nothing?” Seth asked.

Vivian shook her head.

“Are you . . . he . . . uh . . .”

“He’s someone I knew in high school,” Vivian said. “He married my best friend from those days. I’ve seen him maybe twice since my wedding. Christmas cards every year – that kind of thing.”

“And when he was here?”

“He wanted to know about Aaron,” Vivian nodded. “I thought he was being supportive, kind, but I see what you mean. It’s possible he just wanted information from the stupid wife.”

“Did you know anything?”

"No," Vivian said. "One morning, Aaron and I woke up together in our bedroom in the middle of our old life. I got breakfast together and he got dressed. He told me he had a meeting downtown that might screw up the rest of his day. He said he'd call if he was going to be late. He kissed me on the cheek and . . . I never saw or heard from him again. Nothing."

Vivian's eyes glazed over, and she stared at the wall.

"Amelie told me, you know, about Yvonne and witness protection, but I didn't believe her," Vivian said. "How could he do this to me? That's all I thought. I didn't realize . . . and Bella . . . He loved her, more than the others, more than me . . . 'Baby Bell', that's what he called her until she made him stop when she was in high school."

Her head bobbed in a nod and then jerked up to look at him.

"He's going to kill us all," Vivian said.

"He might," Seth said. "He didn't get Yvonne. He doesn't have to kill you."

"What do I do?" Vivian asked.

Seth took a small revolver from his pocket and held it out to her.

"Can you shoot?" he asked.

"I was born and raised in Colorado, Seth. Of course I can shoot," Vivian said. "Amelie made me get a concealed weapon permit when she was at the police academy. Éowyn has been competitive shooting since junior high. She's won a number of awards. Amelie made sure she had a concealed weapon permit as well. Bella too."

Vivian's voice cracked with emotion. She nodded

when she felt under control. He gave her the weapon.

"And Éowyn?"

"That's where they went," Seth said.

"Good," Vivian said.

"This guy," Seth said. "He kills from a distance. You may not have a chance to . . ."

"Then why?" Vivian looked up at him and then nodded. "This is for Jeb."

"I'm afraid so," Seth said.

Vivian checked that the weapon was loaded and the safety was on. She stuck the handgun in her pocket.

"Do you have any idea why Bella went to see my husband?" Vivian asked.

"To confront him," Seth said. "That's what she told Ava."

"And did she?"

"Probably," Seth said what he thought Vivian wanted to hear. "But I don't know."

Vivian nodded. He gave her a box of ammunition. She went to set the box in her suitcase.

"What else can I do?" Vivian asked. "I feel . . . hopeless . . . helpless . . ."

"You can keep your wits about you," Seth said.

"That didn't help Bella."

"No," Seth said. "But she didn't have the luxury of knowing her life was in danger."

"You're sure?"

"If your husband knew his life was in danger, would he have been in that room?"

"Never," Vivian shook her head.

"Keep your wits about you," Seth said. "Keep in touch. I have a friend who lives in Rapid City. A woman. Janet Sales."

He held out a piece of paper with a phone number on it.

"She retired there after twenty years at the Denver PD," Seth said. "Play it off as an old friend, someone you know from here. Call her on the way into town."

"He'll know."

"I doubt it," Seth said. "Everyone counts on you being the clueless wife. It's up to you to decide if you're going to be what everyone expects you to be."

Vivian nodded.

"You have money?"

"Amelie took care of that," Vivian said. "Thank you. Jeb wants me to stay with him, but I convinced him I'd be happier in a hotel."

"I've made your reservations," Seth said. "The address is on the piece of paper. Janet is planning on having dinner with you tonight. If she doesn't hear from you, she'll sound the alarm."

"Good," Vivian said.

"Éowyn will see you to Rapid City," Seth said. "Then she's off. You won't know where Ava or Éowyn are located. That's for your protection."

"But you'll keep them safe?"

"I'll do what I can," Seth said. "The easiest way to get you to give up your location is to convince you something has happened to Éowyn or Ava. If you hear something, call me."

"I don't have a cell phone anymore. Oh," Vivian nodded.

"Right. You don't have one so they can't find you."

"I'll call you from the room," Vivian said. "What are you going to do?"

"I'll try to find the bastard before he finds you," Seth said.

Vivian nodded and zipped her suitcase closed.

"Can you promise me one thing?" Vivian asked.

"Sure."

"If something happens," Vivian said. "Will you take care of Éowyn and Amelie? No matter what. Please."

"I will."

"Good."

The front door bell rang and Vivian adjusted her demeanor to practiced perfect. Seth put the suitcase on the ground, and she wheeled it to the doorway. Dale carried her suitcase down the stairs. Seth followed Vivian to the entryway.

"Jeb, thank you for rescuing me from . . ." Vivian sneered at Seth. " . . . this."

She kissed Jeb's cheek. Over her shoulder, Jeb glanced at Seth. Seth mouthed, "Mother-in-law," and shrugged.

"Come on, Viv," Sheriff Jeb Elliot said. "Let's get you out of here."

Vivian hugged Amelie. With a turn of her head, she left the house. Éowyn followed. Maresol closed the front door.

"What would be good for you?" Seth put his hands

on Ava's shoulders. His eyes were soft and kind.

"Catch a murderer," Ava's eyes shot fire. She spun in place and marched up the stairs.

Chuckling, Maresol went back into the kitchen.

"Are you coming O'Malley, or am I going to have to catch this guy myself?" Ava yelled from his office.

He limped up the stairs.

|-||-|||-||-|||-||-|||-||-|||-||-|||-||-|||-||-|||

FOURTEEN

When the doorbell rang at 2:30 in the morning, Seth looked up at Ava. She raised an eyebrow, smirked, and got up from Mitch's chair. Since her mother and sister had left, they had been working non-stop trying to find Bella's murderer. She had emailed and badgered police departments across the country for parking tickets or other violations around the time when the murders had been committed. Seth had worked his connections to see which property had been sold to the Army. They were definitely making progress. He was confident they would have the killer's name by morning.

Seth got up from his chair and followed Ava to the entryway. She glanced at him, before opening the door. Her old friend, colleague, and FBI forensics mentor Robert

Parrish, also known as Blood Spatter Bob, stood in the doorway. He stepped aside to reveal the three other members of Ava's old laboratory team – Nelson Weeks, Leslie McClintock, and Fran Dekay. They had worked for Ava until she was relieved of duty because her father had used his connections to place her in the job. Collectively, they were also the Denver Police Department's backup forensic laboratory. They had just come off their shift at the lab.

One at a time, her friends held Ava and whispered their condolences. Seth took their coats and hung them on a nearby coat rack. Bob shook Seth's hand.

"Good of you to come," Seth said.

"How is she?" Bob said in a low tone.

"Shut down," Seth said. "Wants to catch a killer first."

Bob nodded. Ava looked up from her conversation with Leslie.

"Please, would you like to come in?" Seth asked.

He made a vague gesture to the house. Bob walked through the kitchen to the den area. Fran went to the kitchen and began digging around in the refrigerator, while Nelson sat down on the couch. Ava stopped to look at a picture of Leslie's six-month-old son on Leslie's phone.

"Maresol left dinner for you," Seth said to Fran. "It's in the oven. She said it should be warm, but to give it a few minutes at 350."

"Great!" Fran turned on the oven and put things back in the refrigerator.

"How did she know we'd be here?" Nelson asked.

"She's a smart lady, but it's not a huge leap," Seth said. "Did you work on the case tonight?"

"Cases," Bob said. "Plus, those marshals?"

"Jasper and Kowalski?" Ava asked.

"Shot each other," Leslie said.

"Or that's what it looks like," Nelson said.

"They're dead?" Seth asked.

"Dead. One of them . . . uh . . ." Leslie squinted and looked at Bob for confirmation. "Jasper?"

"Jasper survived the shooting," Bob said. "Called 911. By the time they got there, he wasn't able to speak. Died in the ambulance on the way to the hospital."

"They have nothing?" Ava's rich voice cracked with fatigue.

"We have something," Fran said. "Don't worry, Ava. They don't fool us. Not for one minute. Now let's eat, and we can discuss all the gory details over dinner."

Ava's colleagues moved to sit at the bar between the kitchen and the den where Fran was setting out their dinner.

"I'm a little surprised you don't know this," Bob said.

"Me?" Seth asked.

"Jasper mentioned your name when he called," Bob said. "Something . . . I wrote it down."

Bob fished around in his pockets for his reading glasses.

"O'Malley," Bob said. "*Tell* or *sell* and then it's garbled."

"I have the recording on my phone," Nelson held

his phone out to Seth.

"They thought he had something to tell you," Fran looked up from where she was plating enchiladas. "But we think it's something you need to let people know."

Seth shrugged and took the phone from Nelson. He played the recording once, and then again.

Both times he heard: "O-mmm-lly, f-s-t . . . eh . . . l." He knew why they thought it was "O'Malley, tell . . . ," but he didn't think they were right. He looked up at Bob and shook his head.

"You're the last person to have had a real conversation with them," Bob said. "The marshals will be here early tomorrow to get you."

"I have a murderer to catch," Seth said. "I can't really spend a day hanging out with them."

"We'll have to be on our way then," Ava said.

Seth's worried eyes flicked to look at her.

"Chicken with no cheese for you," Fran took a small dish out of the oven and gave it to Nelson. "Maresol knows how you feel about cheese."

"Me?" Nelson smiled. "I love cheese. It's just not good for my figure."

Nelson patted his flat, bodybuilder's abs.

"Are you eating?" Fran asked Ava. She shook her head. "Seth?"

"No thanks," Seth said.

"More for us," Bob said.

Ava's lab team fell silent while they ate. When Ava ran the team, they'd eaten dinner here at least once a week. When they were nearly done, Bob cleared his throat.

"We should talk and get out of here," Bob said.

"Right, we don't want to know more than we can testify too," Fran said.

"Exactly," Bob said. "Have you heard from your mother? Sister?"

"So far, so good," Ava said.

"That's a relief," Leslie said.

Nelson, Fran and Bob nodded in agreement.

"Are you still working on the tickets?" Nelson asked.

"I've received information from seventeen cities," Ava said.

"What's this?" Bob asked.

"We're testing Éowyn's idea that over the course of all these years, this guy might have received a parking ticket or a speeding ticket or something, somewhere," Ava said. "You know, one in this city, another in that one. It's a real needle in a haystack."

"Might not pan out," Seth said.

"I have all the paid and unpaid tickets for the weeks before and the week after the murders," Ava said. "It's a lot to get through."

"Why don't you send me what you have?" Nelson asked.

"You're sure?" Ava asked.

"Of course," Nelson said. "It'll only take a half hour or so to see if I can find the same person. I can start it while we talk."

"You should check license plates, in case he had fake IDs," Ava said.

"Make and model," Seth said. "Even if he rents, he's likely to get the same vehicle every time. Something he likes and trusts."

"Sure," Nelson nodded.

"In all the places?" Seth asked.

"Of course," Nelson smiled.

"Nelson was my data geek," Ava said.

"Is," Nelson took his laptop out of his backpack and turned it on. "But I won't ruin the surprise."

"What?" Ava asked.

"Send me the files," Nelson said. Ava jogged out of the room.

"Let's talk murder first, and lab second," Bob said. "I want to get Seth's take on the recording."

"I heard what you heard," Seth said. "And . . . I have a sense that what I hear isn't what he's saying."

"Exactly," Bob said. "Any ideas?"

"None," Seth said. "What do you know about Jasper and Kowalski?"

"They were killed with bullets from each other's Glock 23s," Leslie said. "U.S. Marshal's Service-issued weapons. Ballistics matched their service records."

"Notice any beef between them when you talked to them?" Bob asked.

"No," Seth said. "They seemed like they'd been partners a long time and knew each other well. They moved, and even talked, in sync."

He looked up to make sure Ava was still upstairs.

"They didn't like Alvin much," Seth said. "But I doubt they killed him."

"How did they seem when you talked to them?" Fran asked.

"Angry," Seth said.

"At each other?" Bob asked.

"The situation," Seth said. "They felt bad about Bella. We all do."

With his words, a cloud of sorrow came over them. Leslie looked away. Nelson focused on his computer. Fran went to the sink, and Bob cleared his throat.

"One thing," Seth said. "They had no idea how Bella knew her father was going to be in town. And I don't think they were faking. They were freaked out when she called and even more disturbed when she received permission to see him. We haven't been able to track who approved all of that or how it went down. Jasper and Kowalski were going to do that when they left the hospital."

"You think it was a hit on both of them?" Nelson said.

"Bella didn't just get in the way?" Leslie asked.

"It was a hit," Seth said.

Fifteen

The team fell silent while they focused on the food in front of them.

"What did you find out?" Ava asked as she came back into the room. "I mean, I'm gonna miss Bella for the rest of my life. And my dad? I . . . Anyway, I have a lifetime to feel bad and cry and beat my chest and be mad at God. But I can only find her killer now, before he disappears somewhere. So what can you tell me about her murder?"

"Self-guided bullets," Bob said.

"Military," Leslie said. "*Very* hush, hush, and experimental."

"I found a picture of a test of them on the Internet," Nelson said. "But when I called Sandia National Labs, where the bullets were tested, they kind of freaked out. I was able to find out through a military buddy of mine that they're missing some ammo."

"From Sandia?" Seth asked.

Nelson nodded.

"We were asked to determine how the shooter managed to hit them with such accuracy," Bob said. "He shot through the curtain. There's no evidence of cameras or other surveillance in the room. How did he do it? Everyone assumed he had visual access to the targets. The ammunition implies that he knew where they would be sitting but couldn't necessarily see them."

"Which implicates Jasper or Kowalski," Seth said.

"Right," Bob said.

Seth shook his head.

"What?" Ava asked him.

"They're way ahead of us," Seth said.

"How else would he know where they would be sitting?" Nelson asked.

"I can think of three ways," Seth said. "Satellite imaging, heat, or radar."

"Hacking a satellite isn't easy, but it's definitely doable," Nelson said.

"Or he gained access to the codes when he took this assignment," Seth said.

"He could have stolen the technology from a nearby oil field – sonar, x-ray," Ava said.

"That's right," Fran said. "There are lots of fields out there in the middle of nowhere Colorado."

"Does the Niobrara Shale Field go all the way down there?" Nelson asked.

"No but the Raton Basin is right there," Fran said. "Coal methane and natural gas."

"They'd have stuff like that just lying around or in a trailer," Bob said. "Easy pickings."

"Didn't someone tell you he was a high school science teacher?" Leslie asked.

"Maybe," Seth said.

"We haven't found him yet, Les," Ava said. "He's not on the website and turns out the phone's not answered after the kids are out for the summer. I left a message, but . . ."

"If he's a science teacher, he'd know how to make lots of stuff," Leslie said.

"Good thinking," Seth said. "He could have made something – x-ray or heat or . . ."

"They use these for ghost hunting. My Google search brought up four different of DIY instructions on how to make a thermographic camera," Nelson said. "These would take some amount of skill, but it would be easy for a high school science teacher. There are even instructions for ghost hunters to make one for their iPhones."

He turned the laptop so that Seth could see the screen.

"Can we ask for records to see . . .?" Bob started.

"No time," Seth said.

"He could have used a computer anywhere," Ava said.

"But probably at school," Bob said. "It's worth a try. If Ava kills this guy, we'll have it as backup."

"On it," Nelson said.

"All he needed were the coordinates of where they were sitting," Ava said. "Which he could get from any of these devices?"

"He'd have to get awfully close," Seth said. "He probably knew the layout of the room which would have narrowed his target."

"We'll pass this along," Fran said. "CSI can test it out tomorrow morning."

"Just sent an email," Nelson said.

"Good," Bob said.

"Jasper? Kowalski?" Seth looked at Bob and Leslie. "You have anything?"

"Immediate tox came back negative," Leslie said. "But I sent it on for further testing."

"Franny noticed a kind of lisp . . ." Bob started.

"Slurring," Fran said. "Jasper slurs his words like he's drunk."

"No alcohol or usual suspects in his blood," Leslie said.

"Where were they?" Ava asked.

"Hotel," Bob said. "They had an adjoining room to where . . . uh . . . to their witness. They were filling out paperwork. TV was on like they were watching the game. But CSI wanted us to check if they were drugged."

"And?"

"We agree," Nelson turned his laptop around to show a digital crime scene recreation. "But we think Kowalski was out when he was shot."

"You mean someone knocked them out, came in the room, took Jasper's weapon and shot Kowalski, and then repeated with Jasper?" Ava asked. "Where was CSI? They should have been in the other room all day."

"Break," Fran said. "They were on a break or so they say."

"We think it might be gas," Nelson said. "Put enough in both rooms; CSI gets tired and heads out for caffeine. Knocks these guys out. Bang, bang; grab the gas canisters from the ventilation system; and slip out before anyone notices."

"CSI was standing outside holding Dazbog lattes when the paramedics arrived," Bob said. "They had no idea what was going on."

"Did they test them?" Seth asked.

"Blood and urine for every CSI member," Leslie said. "Clear again. I sent them off to the FBI with the other samples."

"Which brings us to why we're here," Bob said.

Fran, Leslie and Nelson looked up at Ava. Bob cleared his throat.

"What you're up against . . ." Bob shook his head.

"They're way ahead of us," Seth said.

"We want Ava to be safe," Nelson said. "We've interviewed like . . ."

"Forty-two," Fran said.

"Replacements for our Ava," Leslie said. "Some of them are all right, but most of them . . ."

"We want you to come back," Bob said.

"Can't," Ava said. "They took my badge and gun. I'm out."

"The labs are all civilian now," Nelson said. "New

chief. You would have had to choose between being a cop or staying with us."

"What do you mean?" Ava asked. "Why?"

"Because the labs are all civilian-run now," Bob said.

"And it occurred to us that you're a civilian now," Fran said.

"So, will you come back?" Leslie asked.

"What about Bob?" Ava asked. "I'm sure he's doing a great job as your head."

"I retired, Ava," Bob said. "I don't want to deal with the paperwork and politics of running this lab. Plus, the new chief wants us to build teams of people to do backup work for everyone who needs it. Good for him, but my heart's just not there. I want to work on the house, explore blood splatters, and hang out with the grandkids. I'm happy to share what I know, but I don't want to train people. It's a young person's game."

"So, will you take the job?" Nelson asked.

"I'll . . ." Ava's eyes shifted to Seth. He smiled at her. She'd been the head of this crew when he met her. She'd loved her job, her team, and most of all the clean, quiet space of her lab. Ava nodded. "Sure. When do I start?"

"Tomorrow?" Leslie asked.

"When this is settled," Seth's voice was firm.

"But . . ." Ava turned to look at him. Noting the concern on his face, she nodded.

"I think Seth's right," Bob said.

"You can't work on this, anyway," Nelson said. "Conflict of interest and all."

While Ava smiled, her arms slipped around her

middle in a silent hug. Noticing Ava's gesture, Bob got up from his bar stool.

"We should go," Bob said. He walked his dishes to the dishwasher. Fran and Leslie got up.

"What about the recording?" Ava asked.

"Send it to my phone," Seth said. "We're going to have to hit the road. I'll listen to it a few times and see if I can figure it out."

"We wondered . . ." Leslie looked at Fran and fell silent. She put her dishes in the dishwasher. Fran followed her action and the women moved to leave.

"What?" Seth asked. "You wondered what?"

"Why haven't you asked Maresol's psychic friend, Delphie, about all of this?" Fran asked. "Our Ava's life is on the line. Don't you think it might be time?"

"I didn't think of it," Seth said.

"Think of it," Fran said.

Leslie held out her arms and hugged Ava. Fran followed suit. Soon, the lab team was near the door.

"What about my tickets?" Ava asked Nelson.

"Check your email," Nelson said. "Bloom. Parking ticket in Redding in '85; speeding ticket in Syracuse in '03; parking ticket in Beaumont '97. All paid in cash."

"Bloom? Really?" Seth asked.

"Looks like it," Nelson pulled on his jacket. "Parking ticket for Hillery Junior in '85; parking ticket for Hillery the third in '97; a speeding ticket for Hilary in '11."

"You'll let us know about the recording?" Bob asked.

"I will," Seth said.

Bob shook his hand again and followed the rest of the team out the door. When the door closed, the house seemed to emanate still silence. Ava glanced at him. He gave her a soft smile.

"I know what you're thinking," she said. "You think I'm going to break down. You think I'm just avoiding pain. Well, you know what?"

"What?"

"You're right," Ava smiled. "Are you going to call Delphie?"

"In the morning," Seth said.

"Where are we going?" Ava asked.

"To track the Blooms from southern Colorado," Seth said. "We can be in Trinidad in four hours."

"Two if we take the Bugatti," Ava smiled. She had a deep and abiding love for the cobalt blue, ridiculously expensive race car he'd bought at his agent Schmidty's insistence.

"We'd stand out like sore thumbs," Seth said. "We're better off in my truck."

"Fine," Ava said. "But I pick the music."

"All right," Seth said. "You need to shower or change or . . ."

"I'm ready to go," Ava opened the front door and walked out. "You?"

Seth whistled for Clara. When he heard her moving off her favorite spot on his bed, he went to the safe in his hall closet and took out a Glock 20SF handgun. He checked that it was loaded and shoved a full, spare clip into the back pocket of his jeans. Clara stopped to look at him.

He pointed out the door, and Clara trotted after Ava. He set the alarm and followed them out the door.

|-||-|||-||-|||-||-|||-||-|||-||-|||-||-|||-||-|||

Sixteen

They were about fifty miles south of Denver when Ava gave in to sleep. Sleep brought sorrow. Over the course of the last few days, she'd lost her childhood life, her father, and her little sister. With her head in his lap, she wept.

He drove, and she cried. From her perch in the extended cab, Clara rested her head next to Ava's back. Seth stroked Ava's short hair and drove down the front range of the Rocky Mountains on I-25. As he drove, his mind worked to translate the piano piece he heard into notes, stanzas, and tempo. Ava's tears subsided near Walsenburg, and she fell into a deep sleep.

When he reached Trinidad, he pulled off at the motel near the highway and went inside to rent a room. When he returned, Ava and Clara were walking along the grass on the edge of the parking lot. Seth put his arm around her, and they walked in silence.

"I slept," Ava said when they got back to the car. "You didn't."

"I worked on the music," Seth said. "That's better than sleep."

"Is it safe to drive and work on music at the same time?" Ava asked.

"I've done almost everything in my life while working on one piece or another," he said.

Ava raised her eyebrows suggestively. He gave her a knowing nod.

"I never really sleep when I'm working a case," he said. "Would you like to go to the room?"

"Breakfast and killer," she said. "If that's okay?"

"Of course."

"Did you call Delphie?" Ava asked.

"Didn't want to wake you," he said.

"Why don't I shower? You can call," she said.

He nodded and took Clara's leash from the glove compartment of the truck. Connected to the dog, he took Ava's hand, and they went into the motel.

"What is it about a motel room that makes me so horny?" Ava asked when they entered the room. She gave him an enticing smile and began unbuttoning his dress shirt. He pulled off her top and kissed her shoulders and neck. She brought her mouth onto his chest and gasped. In this unguarded moment, her grief caught up with her again.

He negotiated her to the bed, where he lay back and pulled her to him. She clung to him and cried. Ava had insisted for months that she hadn't been affected by her father's betrayal. She was angry for her mother and sisters, but otherwise, she was fine.

Or so she said.

"I'm sorry. I'm sorry. I'm sorry," she said as she tried to catch her breath.

"Everything is fine," he said.

"But . . . we have a motel room and . . ." She sat up to look at him. Her face was red and wet with tears.

"Plenty of years to make good use of motel rooms," Seth said.

She nestled back against him. He held her tight.

"I'm not helping." She sat up straight. "The killer is out there, and I'm blubbering."

"You've been strong for so long," Seth said. "It's all right to feel."

"But . . ." Her tear-strained voice tore at him. "I feel . . . everything. Mad: I'm so mad at my father. Who the hell is he to throw away our whole life? And Mom's no better! Why didn't she know? And then I wonder whether I would know? Would I know?"

Thinking she had asked a rhetorical question Seth didn't respond.

"Would I know?" she asked again.

"Would you know if I was running a chain of prostitution houses?" Seth asked. "Would you know if I was manipulating everything so I could steal another man's wife and keep her as my sex slave? Or . . ."

"Would I know if you were trading away my whole life to . . . I don't know, the Chinese Music Mafia?"

"The Chinese Music Mafia?"

"You know what I mean," Ava said.

"I understand what you mean on so many levels," Seth said.

"And?"

"When you enter a relationship, any relationship, even this relationship, you have to trust yourself first, and then trust the other person about some things," Seth said. "Where do they go when they leave the house? Who are they with? What are they doing?"

"I wouldn't know," Ava said.

"You wouldn't know," Seth said.

Ava nodded. His honesty seemed to ground and reassure her.

"What do I do?" she whispered. "How do I live when I know . . . when I know . . . at any moment . . . this . . .?"

He rolled onto his side to look at her.

"You can look at someone's history," Seth said. "Have they done this type of thing in the past?"

"I don't always know someone's history," Ava said. "I only know what they say."

"Did your father ever hide his 'win-at-any-cost' nature?" Seth asked.

"No," Ava shook her head. "He always had a story of this small person he crushed or that stupid person he tricked or . . . Life was a game which he won by destroying other people."

"There you go," Seth said. "People who value winning at any cost will eventually sell out everyone who loves them in order to come out on top."

"And Bella?" Ava's lip quivered. Knowing what was coming next, he waited to respond. "And Beth?"

At the mention of her murdered best friend, Ava broke down again. Seth pulled her onto his shoulder. They lay together while she cried and the early morning turned into day. They lay together until, without saying another word, Ava got up and went into the bathroom.

"Call Delphie," she said before she closed the bathroom door.

Sitting up, he leaned his elbows on his knees and tried to clear his head. He placed a quick call to McGinty to update him on what had happened so far. He'd just hung up when he heard Ava turn on the water for the shower. He waited a few minutes to be sure she was under the stream of water and called the only true psychic he'd ever met.

Just a couple years younger than Seth, Delphie was a middle-aged flower child who never quite understood how the world worked. She kept bees, wore gauzy floral dresses, and spent most of her summers in her large vegetable garden. For all her weirdness, she was well loved and cared for by her large family and her friends, including Maresol. She'd told him once that he had been her brother in a multitude of past lives. He smiled at the thought.

When the line began to ring, he held the phone away from his ear.

"Seth!" Delphie yelled.

"I can hear," Seth said.

"Oh sorry," Delphie's voice lowered. "I don't know what it is about these things. They seem like they need a good shout."

"Yes," Seth said.

"We've been crazy with worry," Delphie said. "How is Ava?"

"Sad," Seth said.

"I bet," Delphie said. "Do you need some help with the case?"

"I do," Seth said.

"Great!" Delphie yelled. "Oh sorry. I'm happy I finally get to help. You know I try not to interfere and . . ."

"It's all right," Seth said.

"Good," Delphie said. "What do you need?"

"What can you tell me?" Seth asked.

"First, you're on the right track," Delphie said. "I don't know why, but I keep seeing flowers."

"Bloom?"

"Yep, that's it," Delphie said.

"Have you seen a U.S. marshal around?" Seth asked.

"I don't know any U.S. marshals," Delphie said.

"Ghosts."

"Oh," Delphie said. "No, what's his name?"

"Jasper," Seth said.

"Full name, Seth."

"Uh," Seth searched the recesses of his mind. "No idea. He was just killed. Is his murder in the paper?"

"Let me look," Delphie said. He heard the door to her apartment open, and the soft thump of her bare feet as she walked down the hallway. Delphie lived in a private apartment with most of her extended family in an enormous old home in Uptown Denver that they called the

Castle. He heard her flip through the Denver Post. "Here it is. Reginald Jasper, U.S. Marshal. Oh hello. He's quite handsome."

He waited while Delphie chatted with the spirit.

"What would you like to know?" Delphie asked.

"I think he left me a message," Seth said. "It was garbled."

"I don't know, Seth," Delphie whispered. "When people first die, they rarely remember . . . Oh yeah? Okay, I'll tell him."

"What did he say?"

"He said father; son; daughter," Delphie said. "Does that mean anything to you?"

Seth reviewed the recording in his mind. He could see how "f-s-t" could easily be "f-s-d" or father, son, daughter. He nodded and then realized that she couldn't see him.

"Yes," Seth said.

"He's getting quite agitated," Delphie said. "Don't worry, I'll tell him. Yes, you can go."

"What was that?"

"He says the police think he killed his partner, and that they killed their witness," Delphie said. "Was that Ava's father?"

"Yes."

"Oh," Delphie said. "I'm right in the middle of everything."

"Yes."

"Okay," Delphie said. "That's okay. I can help. I like to help. That's really good."

"Did he kill his partner?"

"Oh right," Delphie chuckled. "No, he didn't, and they weren't involved in killing Ava's father or her sister. You can't talk to her sister, because she's moved on."

"That seems fast," Seth said.

"She had a little help," Delphie's voice pinched.

"You sent her on?"

"I felt bad for her, and . . . well . . . she is Ava's sister. I'd do it for you."

"And her father?"

"I've never wanted anything to do with that man," Delphie's voice was hard. Delphie and Maresol were good friends with Yvonne Smith, the woman Aaron Alvin had held as a sex slave. "But Ava is lovely. Everyone's been asking about her. She's well loved. How is she doing?"

"She's . . ."

"Seth!" Delphie squeaked. "Ava's mother. Her mother and sister. Older sister. Seth! They are not safe!"

"I thought so," Seth said.

"But . . . now . . ." Delphie stopped talking. Used to her fits and starts, Seth waited for her to circle back to him. "It's a good thing you gave Vivian that gun."

"And Éowyn?"

"She'll meet her one and only love today," Delphie said with certainty. "The next few hours are very dangerous for them, but there's a good chance that they'll be fine. You should call your criminal defense lawyer. They *might* need her. But . . . maybe not."

"I will," Seth said. "And the killers?"

"You'll find them exactly where you expect to,"

Delphie said. “But watch out, Seth. Ava is in real danger.”

“Why?”

“Because he’ll sneak up on you when you least expect it,” Delphie said. “Four times two. That’s the agreement. He’ll honor that agreement.”

“What?” Seth raised his voice in frustration.

“I don’t know what it means,” Delphie’s voice was defensive. “This is your life, Seth O’Malley. If you don’t know what I’m talking about, then maybe you should do something about your life.”

Sixteen

Seth took a deep breath to calm his frustration. He and Delphie always got to this place. Maresol told him once that Delphie only spoke what was told to her; she never interpreted what was said. She thought that people who interpreted interfered with forces beyond their control and manipulated the truth. He just wished she would tell him what everything meant. But Delphie never told him. He heard Delphie laugh at him.

"I know, I know," he said.

"Just tell me," Delphie mimicked his voice. He laughed.

"Anything else?" he asked.

"Not that I can think of," Delphie said. "Take care of yourself, Seth. This is a big, big mess. Bigger than you or me. A big mess. You're cleaning up a lot of karma. And when it's over, a lot of good people can finally rest."

"Okay, thanks," Seth said. He was about to hang up when he heard her voice.

"And Seth?"

"Yes?"

"Chamber a round," Delphie said. "Do you know what that means? Because it doesn't mean anything to me."

"Yes," Seth took the handgun from his jacket pocket.

"Good," Delphie said. "Blessings."

She hung up.

Seth took the handgun out of his jacket pocket and snapped a bullet into the chamber. Clara looked up at him.

"Just a precaution," he said to the dog.

He was about to tuck the weapon into the back band of his jeans when he heard his army captain's voice ring in his head repeating what he'd always said, "Wanna shoot yourself in the ass, O'Malley?"

"No, I don't," Seth said out loud. He'd have to wait to get his holster from the car.

"Talking to yourself," Ava said when she came out of the bathroom. Her flawless nakedness held his full attention. "What did Delphie say?"

"We should get breakfast downtown and go hunt us a killer," Seth said.

"That's oddly clear for Delphie," Ava smirked.

"Want to start over?" he asked.

"I do . . . I . . . I just can't," Ava said. "Is that okay?"

"That's okay," Seth smiled to assure her. "Do you

think your lab buddies will be awake?"

"Leslie and Fran?" Ava asked. "They have kids to take care of."

"Hmm," Seth said. His eyes followed her movements. She leaned over to take a pair of clean underwear from her purse and slipped them on.

"Why?" Ava asked while she pulled on her jeans.

"I wondered if I could look at the security tape from the hotel," Seth said.

"Huh," Ava said. "They didn't mention a security video. I bet they've looked at it though. Every big hotel has cameras in the corridors."

Seth nodded.

"You could call Ferg," Ava said. With her bra around her waist, she walked into the bathroom. "He's usually on until at least eight."

Seth called his old friend Captain Ferguson of the Denver Police. He, Mitch, and Ferg had come through the ranks around the same time. Captain Ferguson was the best crime scene investigator Seth had ever worked with. Ferg had the ability to see things almost no one else could, and he was able to interpret what they meant. He was also a good, loyal friend.

"Ferg?" Seth asked.

"Hey," Captain Ferguson said. "Yeah, I'm going to be late again. You know things are pretty hot here."

Seth listened while Ferg walked somewhere private.

"Go," Ferg said.

"I'd like to see the security tape from the hotel," Seth said.

"There's a real shit storm here. Alvin's dead. Marshals are dead. We're clueless," Ferg said. "And some dick named O'Malley has gone missing. They're looking all over for him. His housekeeper suddenly doesn't speak English, and that kid who lives with him is stupider than usual. But what I want to know is . . ."

Seth heard what sounded like a closet door close.

"Where is my Ava?" Ferg whispered.

"Safe," Seth said. "For now."

He listened while Captain Ferguson caught his breath. Ferg had been one of Ava's supervisors. He loved her like a daughter. When Seth and Ava had started dating, Ferg had cornered Seth to make sure his intentions were good. Seth heard Ferg walking with the phone again.

"Well, you don't have to be a bitch," Ferg said, and the line went dead.

Seth waited a few minutes and checked his phone. Ferg sent him an email with a link to the surveillance video. While he didn't own a super-fancy phone, this phone had been issued to him by the Denver Police Department. It was "smart" enough to get email, and photos, and play videos. He moved the cursor to around the time when the marshals were killed and put on his headphones.

There was a cleaning cart in the hallway. In a large hotel, there was probably always a cleaning cart in the hallway. He backed up the video. A corner of the cleaning cart appeared about an hour before the marshals were killed. Although he couldn't see her or the cart, he heard the cleaning woman say, "Housekeeping," in a thick, South American accent, and a tap on the door. Fifteen minutes later, the cart moved forward, and the cleaning woman came into view. She was fairly small and thin. She had dark-hair and ruddy but fair skin. She moved with ease down the hallway, cleaning the rooms. She was cleaning the room next door to the marshals when they were killed. Seth counted on his fingers and called Ferg.

"Check room 374," Seth said.

"And why is that?"

"You'll find a dead cleaning woman in it," Seth said.

"We checked out the cleaning woman," Ferg said.

"You checked out a woman you thought was the cleaning woman," Seth said. "Did you keep her cart?"

"Yes," Ferg said.

"The actual cleaning woman is either in 374 or in the cart," Seth said. "Someone's mother didn't come home from work yesterday."

"Motherfu . . ." Ferg slammed the phone down.

"What was that?" Ava said.

She'd covered her tear-stained face with a light application of makeup. He kissed her cheek, and she sat down to put on her running shoes.

"Ferg," Seth said.

"You found something?"

"I think so," Seth said. "Seems like we have a family of killers."

"We knew that," Ava said.

"This is a family job," Seth said. "That's what Jasper was trying to say – father; son; daughter. The daughter, disguised as housekeeping staff, killed the marshals."

"Wow," Ava said.

Seth nodded.

"I'm starving," Ava said.

"Yes. Let's eat," Seth said. "I'd love some coffee."

"You going to tell me what Delphie said?" Ava asked.

Rather than answer, he signaled Clara, and they left the room to find breakfast.

|-||-|||-||-|||-||-|||-||-|||-||-|||-||-|||-||-|||

Eighteen

Seth set down his coffee cup and smiled at Ava. Her sorrow had left her cheeks flushed and her lips, red and full. The southern Colorado morning sun cast her in a beautiful light. Noticing his look, she cocked her head to the side in a "What?" He cupped her face with his left hand and stroked the scar on her cheek. She closed her eyes and rested her chin in his hand.

He hadn't thought he'd find love again. He certainly never thought he'd have any kind of relationship with someone so much younger. But here he was, sitting in a small diner in the middle of downtown Trinidad, Colorado, looking at the young woman who'd stolen his heart. She gave him a soft smile.

"How's your breakfast?" she nodded toward his

pancakes.

He shrugged.

"And coffee?"

"Hot, watery, and plentiful."

"Sounds like Seth's perfect coffee," Ava said. "I thought we could . . ."

His phone rang. He turned the phone over to look at it; she nodded that he should answer.

"O'Malley."

He heard the sound of wind and the clip-clop of fast-moving horses.

"Sir, it's Switch," a man's voice yelled. His voice held the echo of a Bluetooth headset.

"Go," Seth said.

Sergeant First Class Gardner "Switch" Thomas was the current caretaker of his family homestead outside of Granby.

"Came at dawn. But holy Christ . . ." Seth heard the horses slow down. There was a splashing sound as they forded the river, and then the horses sped up again. Switch yelled, "Go in front."

"Switch?"

"Who is this girl?" Switch asked. Seth smiled. "Last night, I thought I was ready to kill her. She's such a bitch."

Seth heard Éowyn yell something.

"That's right, I called you a bitch," Switch laughed. Seth heard Éowyn laugh. "Did you know she was a high school champion? College marksman? Was on the team in college and law school. We even competed against each other five years ago. Said she rooted for me in Beijing."

"What happened this morning?"

"Shooter came just before dawn," Switch said. "We were arguing in the kitchen by the sink. I'd made coffee and she thought it was crap. She's on your horse by the way."

Seth heard the horses begin to gallop as the sound of their hooves echoed off the granite cliffs at the edge of the lower pasture. The homestead was his older brother Saul's favorite place on the planet. Seth knew the land like the back of his hand.

"What happened?" Seth repeated.

"She saw the guy first. Grabbed the shotgun. The one on the wall," Switch said. "Bam. Bam. Shot out the kitchen window."

"You pushed me," Éowyn gave an indignant shout.

"Guy clipped me. Caught me in right upper arm."

"And?"

"You need to call Granby PD. She made a quality field dressing, I can say that for her, and . . ." Switch yelled to Éowyn. "Right at the cairn. No, your other right."

"Did you get him?"

"What do you think?" Switch laughed. "Left-handed. Even impressed little miss 'I-can-shoot-better-than-you-any-day-anyhow' Annie Oakley."

Seth heard Éowyn laugh.

"She insisted on taking your horse," Switch said. "I thought it was too big for her but . . ."

"Too big for you, maybe," Éowyn's voice was hard and edgy, but Seth heard a feminine giggle mixed in with her words. Remembering what Delphie's had said, Seth smiled.

"You don't need to be talking like that," Switch said.

Éowyn yelled something Seth couldn't hear. Switch laughed.

"Listen," Switch said. "She says you're her 'Sugar Daddy.' I just want to know . . ."

"She's Ava's sister," Seth said. "Be nice."

"Good to know," Switch said. "We're heading to the hideout in the Upper Pasture. But you got to call and have 'em come pick up the body."

"Did you call your command?"

"Before we left. I'll check in when we get there," Switch said. "You think there'll be another?"

"Might be," Seth said. "Turns out there are three shooters. Two now."

"We're armed," Switch said. "And dangerous. Out."

He heard Éowyn laugh and the line went dead.

"What was that?" Ava asked.

"They came for Éowyn," Seth said.

Ava gasped.

"She's with Switch," Seth said.

"You sent her to Switch?" Ava's eyebrows shot straight up. "And?"

"I think it's love."

"I thought he was . . ." Ava's head shifted back and forth to indicate that he might be gay.

"That's one of the reasons he's called Switch," Seth said.

"What's the other?" Ava smiled.

"He can shoot equally well with both hands," Seth

said. "Ambidextrous."

"He's not really her type," Ava said. "She likes dark-haired, blue-eyed, super-handsome sociopaths in expensive suits."

Switch had received the worst of his mother's extreme whiteness and his father's deep blackness. He wore his tan-colored hair long and kinky, like a blonde steel wool pad on top of his head. He'd grown up with his father and spoke in an almost unintelligible Southern drawl. He dressed mostly in fatigues, even when he wasn't at work as a marksmanship instructor at Fort Carson. Seth doubted he owned a suit.

"I don't think he's a sociopath," Seth said. "Those guys usually go work for Black Ops."

"You watch, she'll remake him," Ava said. "Clothing, face, and that hair."

"I'm sure she'll try," Seth smiled.

"So Éowyn's met her match?" Ava laughed.

Seth nodded.

"Is she all right?" Ava asked.

"Sassy and controlling. What's that tell you?"

"She's scared. She gets like that when she's scared," Ava said. "Where are they going?"

"I'm not quite sure," Seth said.

Ava's eyes slipped over his face. Seeing his lie to protect her, she nodded. It was safer for her if she didn't know.

"She's safe?"

"There's Switch to worry about."

Ava smiled and turned her attention to her

breakfast. Her shoulders squared with tension. The moment of love and safety had passed.

"We're going to catch this guy before . . .?"

"I sure hope so," Seth said.

He took out his wallet and put enough cash on the table to cover their meal and the tip.

"Ready?" He drained his coffee cup.

She nodded. Standing, he took her hand and they left the restaurant.

|-||-|||-||-|||-||-|||-||-|||-||-|||-||-|||-||-|||

Nineteen

"What do you think?" Seth asked.

They were sitting in the parking lot of Hoehne High School. The principal had agreed to see them if they made it before noon.

"It's worth a try," Ava said.

Seth got out of the truck and went around to open Ava's door. His eyes scanned the horizon. He'd picked the high school because he thought it was unlikely that the shooter would target them there. Hopefully, they could find out everything they needed and be on their way before anything happened.

"What is it?" Ava asked.

"Nothing," Seth said.

"You've been odd and pensive ever since you talked

to Delphie," Ava said.

"Pensive?"

Ava chuckled at his tone. She stopped walking. He turned and instinctively scanned the area again. Surprised, she looked around.

"They're coming for me," Ava said. "That's what you didn't say."

Seth nodded.

"Did Delphie say if I . . ."

"She didn't," Seth said. "I don't think that's been determined yet."

"And Mom? Éowyn?"

"She said they were in danger but would be fine," Seth said. "Listen, we need to get inside or . . ."

"Get out of the open," Ava nodded. They jogged to the building. "Why didn't you tell me?"

"Because we can only live this moment and the next," Seth said. "Our lives are determined by our actions."

"I'm not a child," Ava said. "I've won plenty of marksmanship awards and . . ."

She glanced at him.

"What can I say?" Seth stopped to open the school door. "I'm an old-fashioned pig. You knew that."

She smiled, and he held the door for her. She stopped short, and he ran into her.

"Love you, piggy," she whispered in his ear. He nuzzled her neck and his phone rang.

"O'Malley?" the voice on the phone asked.

"You've got him," Seth said.

"Deputy Young, Grant County Sheriffs," the man

said. "You called about a white male shot on the edge of your property."

"Yes," Seth said.

"Driver's license Hillery Bloom Jr.," Deputy Young said. "Age 82 years. Has a rifle that matches the hollow points stuck in the wall of your kitchen. Shot twice in the head with what looks like the M9 on your kitchen counter. I've got an MP from Fort Carson breathing down my neck. Does any of this sound familiar?"

"Yes," Seth said. "Call Denver PD and the U.S. marshals."

"Turns out I don't have to work that hard," Deputy Young said. "U.S. marshals arrived just after we did. Something about two dead marshals, that prick, Aaron Alvin, and a missing Seth O'Malley?"

"Sounds like you have everything under control," Seth said. "Can you do me a favor?"

"You can ask," Deputy Young said.

"Can you keep this out of the press?" Seth asked.

"No problem," Deputy Young said. "We just had a report of some gunfire on that dick O'Malley's land. Who wouldn't believe that?"

Seth laughed.

"And Seth?"

"Jethro?"

"You've got twenty-four hours before I put out an APB on Switch."

Seth heard a man swear rapid-fire at Deputy Young.

"Did you really have to call in the Fort?" Deputy

Young asked.

"Didn't," Seth said.

"Makes you wonder," Deputy Young said. "You gonna tell me where they are?"

"Hideout," Seth said.

The Deputy chuckled and hung up.

"What was that?" Ava asked.

"Friend of my older brother's," Seth said. "They found the guy Switch shot. Hillery Bloom Jr."

"The father," Ava said.

"Switch shot Gramps in the head," Seth said.

"One down," Ava said and started walking down the hall. "Two to go."

He paused for a moment. It was really five down. Aaron Alvin, Bella, and the two marshals were dead. The attempt on Éowyn made five down with three to go. With every passing moment, Ava's brush with death came closer. His heart squeezed with anxiety.

"Coming?" Ava smiled at him from the doorway to the principal's office.

Seth nodded and followed her into the office. They stood in the entryway and tried to get their bearings. Outside of what looked like a brand new world map, the office didn't look like it had been updated in a decade. It looked as if all the people who worked in this office were either at lunch or had fled the building.

"Hello?" Ava asked.

"Be right there!" a man's voice called from somewhere in the back.

Seth put his hand on his handgun and his other

arm around Ava. She rested her head on his shoulder.

"Hey! You must be O'Malley," A thirty-something man with a big smile came from a back office. "Seth, right?"

Seth held out a hand for him to shake.

"Got your message. My staff is out for break, and I'm trying to work the copy machine. Damn budget cuts. We have to account for every sheet, and I can never remember my number."

He brightened when his eyes fell on Ava.

"This is Ava." Unsure of whether to use her last name, "Alvin," he glanced at her.

"Ava O'Malley," she smiled and shook the principal's hand.

"You wouldn't happen to know . . .?" he asked her.

"I can try," Ava said.

"The numbers on this sticky," the principal pointed to a bright-colored note stuck to the page.

She took the sheet from the principal and went back into the equipment room. Seth's worried eyes followed her before turning to the principal.

"You wanted to get some information about our science department?" the principal asked. "You police?"

"Why?"

"You look like police," the principal said.

Seth shrugged.

"Anyway, we have two science teachers," the principal said. "You want to see their classrooms?"

"Sure," Seth's eyes went to where Ava had gone.

"You can leave your daughter here," the principal said.

"What can you tell me about Hillery Bloom?" Seth asked.

"Bloom?" the principal looked surprised. "He was the science teacher here for . . . gosh, a long time. Started way before my time. The kids really liked him. He always had some crazy experiment for them to try. Man, I'll tell you, did I get phone calls from parents about that guy. 'We went to the drive in and child put a candy in his coke. It blew up in the car.' Stuff like that."

"You're using the past tense," Seth said.

"He didn't teach last year," the principal said. "He's got some kind of autoimmune kidney thing. He said it was from the Army maneuver site; reaction to some nerve gas or something like that. Their land is right on the border of Piñon Canyon. They're big 'save-the-land-from-the-evil-Army' people."

The principal nodded.

"You didn't like him much," Seth said.

"I . . ." The principal blushed and didn't respond.

"How come?" Ava asked. She gave the principal a big smile and handed him his copy.

"Thanks," the principal looked at her. "I was just telling your dad . . ."

"Husband," Ava said.

"Oh. Sorry," the principal blushed. She gave him a bright smile.

"It's an easy mistake," Seth said.

"I . . . yeah." The principal shifted back and forth on his feet. "You're right. I don't like him. He and his family are big 'no-tax' anti-government people."

"No tax? Isn't he a school teacher?" Ava asked.

"Right," the principal said. "He doesn't believe in state property taxes. Didn't matter that state property taxes pay for schools, even his salary, his medical insurance, or his retirement. And he wasn't like 'everyone has to pay property taxes.' It was like the state personally cursed him and his family with the blight of property taxes. Or that's how he acted."

"Kind of odd," Seth said.

"Odd," the principal said. "The guy had a screw loose. They ranch close to a hundred thousand acres out of Houghton. They homesteaded the land after the Civil War. 'Crawled up from Texas after the battle at Palmito Hill,' that's what he always said, anyway. The land was pretty much worthless until the Army wanted to expand. Soon as there was an actual buyer for the land, the assessor increased the tax value of the place. I mean, that's just how land works; it gets more valuable when more people want it. Not to Bloom. He was furious when his taxes went up. That was just before he got sick."

"Do you have his medical records?" Ava smiled.

"For his leave?" the principal shifted back and forth uncomfortably again. "Um . . . I'd get in big trouble if anyone found out I . . ."

"We won't tell," Ava said. "I'd just like to take a look."

"Why?" the principal asked.

"Just curious." Ava gave him a beautiful smile.

The principal flushed. He glanced at Seth and went to a cabinet. He dug through a drawer of folders and gave her one. Ava took it and sat down in the secretary's chair.

"I have to say," the principal said. "He's real sick. He spent most of last summer in the hospital . . . uh . . . in Albuquerque, I think. I do know he went up to Denver to that allergy hospital."

"National Jewish?" Seth asked.

"That's the one," the principal leaned into Seth. "I'll tell you, though. His doctor told me that he didn't think he was sick from some Army thing. He thought it was . . ."

The principal looked around to make sure no one was there.

"Inbreeding," the principal nodded. "Those old ranch families out there have been inter-marrying since they moved here. And the treatment? Something simple like taking a pill or something."

"Is he on disability now?" Seth asked.

"Trying for it," the principal said. "I'd never say this to anyone else, but I'll tell you it really pisses me off that he's all up in arms about paying his taxes and now wants disability. But Bloom says he was cursed by the U.S. Army. 'The U.S. government should pay.' That's what he says; like he's not a U.S. citizen or something."

"I heard they sold to the Army," Seth said.

"Probably to move into town for his medical treatments," the principal said. "We graduated his oldest in May. Those girls . . ."

The principal shook his head.

"Sounds like you'll be glad to be rid of the lot of them," Seth said.

"You said that, not me," the principal said.

Seth smiled.

"Did he have access to a computer?" Ava said.

She walked toward them and held out the file. The principal grabbed the file and jammed it back in the drawer.

"Computer?" the principal asked. "Not here. Too paranoid. We have a strict policy on computer use for teachers and students. We have a guy who reviews everything and we turn any suspicious computer use over the Homeland Security. We have a few federal grants and that's part of getting the money."

"He wouldn't happen to be a ghost hunter, would he?" Seth asked.

The principal turned to look at Seth and then shook his head.

"That's weird," the principal said. "How did you know that?"

"Lucky guess," Seth said. "Why?"

"He was big into reconstructing the Civil War," the principal said. "Every summer, he'd load up his entire family and take them to some Civil War battlefield in Alabama or Georgia or wherever. They'd do paranormal investigations to get information from the soldiers' ghosts. Helps them in their recreations of the battles. That's what I mean. Who does that kind of crap?"

"A lot of people are fascinated," Seth said.

"Send 'em to Iraq," the principal said. "Two tours with the Colorado Guard cured me of any interest in war. You ever go?"

"First Infantry," Seth said. "Caught the end of

Vietnam."

"Yeah? My old man was on a bomber crew over Laos. Where were you?"

"Cu Chi."

"Tunnel rat?"

"Something like that," Seth said.

"They have guys in tunnels in Afghanistan," the principal said.

"Marines," Seth said. "I met a few a couple of years ago. At least they don't have to deal with Agent Orange showers."

"Shit, you really are a rat," the principal said. "Lots of guys say they went down but . . . Then you know what I mean."

"I know what you mean," Seth said.

"You still want to see the science rooms?" the principal asked.

"We're mostly looking for Bloom," Ava said.

"He used to make a lot of his ghost hunting gear here," the principal said.

"Did you ever see it?" Ava asked.

"Sure," the principal said. "The school newspaper highlighted his ghost hunting adventures. There's a picture . . ."

The principal went to his secretary's desk, logged in, and looked around.

"Here's a photo," he clicked on the picture. "This was taken right after he got back from Denver."

"When was that?" Seth pointed to a long-distance thermographic camera. Ava nodded.

"Early fall," the principal said. "Thought he was better. He came to work, got sick, came back, and then took leave. This was around Halloween."

"Can I have a copy of the photo?" Ava asked.

"If you can figure out how to print it," the principal said.

"Sure," Ava said.

The principal stepped away from the computer, and Ava sat down in the secretary's chair.

"We're going to pass this information on to the Denver Police," Seth said. "They'll probably call."

"Sure," the principal said. "You won't tell them about looking at the records, or that I don't like Bloom or the disability thing or . . ."

"We won't," Seth said.

"What's he supposed to have done?" the principal asked.

"Killed a few people," Seth shrugged.

"Shot them?" the principal asked. "Bloom has a shooting range on his land. I've heard he's a great shot. He was always after me to come out to the range, but you know how it is."

"Shooting people cures your desire to shoot targets?"

"You think I'll ever get over that?" the principal asked.

"No," Seth said. "You won't."

"Did you?"

"Never," Seth said.

"Have you had to shoot people since . . .?"

"Yes," Seth said. "But I'm not a high school principal. You're smarter than I was."

Reassured, the principal nodded.

"You wouldn't know if he has any friends who work at Sandia National Laboratory, would you?" Ava asked. She folded over the photo of Bloom's thermographic camera and stuck it in the back pocket of her jeans.

"In Albuquerque?" the principal asked. "Sure. His wife, Meldy, works there. Or did until he got sick."

"Kind of a long commute," Seth said.

"Four hours or so," the principal said. "She's home on the weekends."

"But?"

"They never seemed that close," the principal said. "I was kind of surprised when she quit work because he was sick."

"Marital problems?" Ava asked.

"Different species," the principal put his hand over his mouth. "Did I say that out loud?"

"I know what you mean," Seth smiled.

"She was lovely, funny, friendly, and smart," the principal said. "He and his dad ran the ranch. She and the girls were the outsiders. They rarely went on those summer vacations. The girls stayed with their mom in Albuquerque."

Nodding, Seth held out his hand. The principal shook it.

"You've been very helpful," Seth said.

"You really think he killed some people?" the principal asked.

"More than fifty or sixty," Seth said.

"What?" the principal asked.

"Don't listen to him," Ava said. "He's been gloomy all day. Thanks for your help!"

"Thank you," Seth nodded.

Ava took Seth's arm, and they left the principal's office. Seth slipped his arm around her, and they walked to the truck. He unlocked her door then pinned her against it. She put her arms around his neck. For a moment, all the madness slipped away. She kissed him. In her sweet kiss, he felt equal doses of her confusion and her love for him. He stroked her cheek.

"I like the sound of you calling me your husband," Seth said. "Ava O'Malley."

"Me too," Ava smiled and got into the truck.

He went around and got in the driver's side.

"Where to?" Ava asked.

"Piñon Canyon," Seth said. "See a man about some Army land."

"Anyone there?" Ava asked.

"Said he would be," Seth said. "Even got a pass for Clara."

"When do we have to be there?"

"Couple of hours, I guess," Seth said. "I figured you'd want to send the photo to your lab."

"Let's stop at the motel," Ava gave him a saucy smile. "Fax this in and catch up."

"Sounds good," Seth started the truck.

|-||-|||-||-|||-||-|||-||-|||-||-|||-||-|||-||-|||

Twenty

Seth reached over to hold Ava's hand as he turned into Piñon Canyon Maneuver Site. She kissed his cheek. After asking the front desk to fax the photo, they'd made quiet, soft love. As if she was savoring the experience, storing it up for a later memory, she had moved with great care. She'd held onto him with all her might when she climaxed. He held her when her grief caught up to her, and she sobbed.

He glanced at her. He'd always known that these revelations about her father would change her and, in turn, their life. Driving along the empty highway, his mind knew what his heart refused to see; she was slowly saying good-bye.

"Love you," he said, after giving their driver's licenses to the guard at the gate. She kissed his lips and smiled. "Are you sure you're all right with all of this?"

"I'm glad to be here," Ava said. "Grateful. You don't have to include me. You don't even have to be investigating all of this. But here you are, doing what you do best, for me. Thanks."

"Go straight ahead, Mr. O'Malley," the guard said and gave back their driver's licenses. "You'll need to transfer vehicles, and they will take you to the property in question."

The guard saluted him and he nodded.

"What was that?" Ava asked as he drove forward.

"What?"

"The salute?" Ava asked.

"I don't know," Seth smiled at her. "Maybe he liked my good looks."

Ava laughed but gave him a strong "Tell me" look.

"I used to work on a team that looked for MIAs in Vietnam, Laos, and other places," Seth said. "I got into it to find Saul."

He pulled into another parking lot.

"Your older brother?" Ava asked.

"He was in a camp in Laos," Seth said.

"Did you find him?"

"I was too late," Seth said. "But yes, I found him. Scattered his ashes on the homestead and later with Mom – the two things he loved. My record identifies me as a member of that team."

"You're still on the team?" Ava asked.

A fast-moving, sand-camouflaged Humvee came over a hill and flew in their direction.

"It's the kind of thing you don't get out of," Seth said. "If my country needs me, my love, I will answer her call."

"I like that about you," Ava said.

She slid across the bench seat to sit next to him. He put his arm around her. With her head on his shoulder, they waited for the Humvee. The vehicle disgorged two Army sergeants with machine guns. The Sergeants frisked them for weapons and cameras. After negotiating, they agreed to leave their phones in the truck, but Seth kept his handgun. Clara hopped in the back of the Humvee and they followed.

With the snow-tipped Sangre de Cristo mountain range in the background, the Humvee zoomed over the dry prairie and grassy hills of the Maneuver site. On their right, a large military action was unfolding with tanks, helicopters, and men on foot. Out on the horizon, a few stick-figure soldiers seemed to be working their way through a mock village.

The Humvee came to an abrupt stop at a helicopter pad. They waited while a large military helicopter descended. Seth moved to sit in the back with Clara so that the U.S. Army deputy general counsel for Piñon Canyon, Richard Sarkasian, could get in the Humvee. They took off again.

Seth couldn't hear what Richard was saying over the sound of the Humvee, but it looked like he introduced himself to Ava. Richard glanced at Seth when he realized Ava was the daughter of the recently deceased former Colorado attorney general Aaron Alvin. The lawyer adjusted his demeanor to both sympathetic and serious. The Humvee jerked to a stop again.

"I thought you'd like to see what we're talking about," Richard said.

Seth and Ava followed him out of the Humvee. Seth let Clara off her leash, and she zoomed off after a prairie dog. Richard walked a few feet and stopped on a ridge overlooking the black asphalt of Highway 350.

"That's the land," Richard said. "The Bloom's ranch is in two parcels – from here to the Apishapa Game Management Area and another section on the other side. Water rights too."

"Seems big," Seth said.

"In total, it's close to ninety thousand acres of prime ranch land," Richard said. "The family homesteaded a few sections, four or five I think, and then bought the rest. They got the bulk of it during the dustbowl, bought out their neighbors for pennies, then picked up a section here or there when it was available."

"Cattle land?" Seth asked.

"Primarily," Richard said. "We paid them every single penny the land was worth, and then some."

"Sounds expensive," Seth said.

"Oh yeah," Richard said.

"Who'd you deal with?" Ava asked.

"Hillary Bloom, the daughter, mostly," Richard said. "She made an enormous drama about how her father got sick from what we were doing out here. Look around you."

Richard gestured for them to look.

"We haven't done shit on this edge of the property, probably ever," Richard said. "Too exposed."

"Seems odd to have an eighteen-year-old do the negotiations," Seth said.

"She just ran the numbers and the papers," Richard said. "When it got down to the nitty-gritty, I dealt with Hillery the third."

Richard grimaced.

"Didn't like him?" Ava asked.

"The man is a python," Richard said. "Sick my ass. I don't know what they're up to, but that man was as robust as I am."

Seth glanced at Ava. He'd forgotten to ask her about Bloom's medical records. She winked to acknowledge his oversight.

"I'll tell you," Richard said. "I wouldn't want to be caught in a dark alley with either one of them. They look normal, but there's something just not right there. The daughter's better than the father, but she may have just not grown into herself yet."

"There's some evidence that they have a genetic mutation," Ava said.

"I'd believe it," Richard said.

Seth pointed to a truck turning onto Highway 350 from the ranch.

"I thought you bought it," Seth said.

"They refused to let us have it until August," Richard said. "You know how hot it is here in August? I can't shake the feeling that they did it just to be contrary. We're so desperate for the land that we'll do whatever they ask."

"Looks like they're still living there," Ava said.

Richard scowled and turned away from the highway. They followed him down the rise.

"Bloom tried to swing a confidentiality agreement on the sale," Richard said. "Ranchers around here are still sore about the Army opening this site. Bloom didn't want his neighbors to know he sold out. But . . ."

Richard shrugged.

"Can't have everything you want?" Seth asked.

"You can't take tax dollars and keep it confidential. Maybe in the '50s but not now," Richard shook his head. "They also wanted us to fund the deal now but they'd stay on the property until August. That didn't fly either. And honestly? I don't trust 'em. It wouldn't surprise me at all if we get there in August and find they've done what they could to make the land unusable for us. Wouldn't surprise me a bit."

Richard walked back to the Humvee and opened the door to the back seat. He turned to Seth and Ava.

"Makes you wonder," Richard said.

"What?" Ava asked.

"Why do they need all that money now?" Richard asked. "Army Intelligence worked up a deep background on them. Hillery the third is sick, but he has good medical coverage through the state teacher's union. The family isn't in debt. The wife makes great money at Sandia, even on leave. Why sell?"

"Why indeed?" Seth asked.

Just then a breeze blew across the highway, down

the rise, and straight up Seth's back. Turning around to look at the ranch, he felt an overwhelming sense that something horrible had happened there. He nudged Ava forward and she got into the Humvee. The deputy general counsel followed. Seth took one last look across the highway, felt an involuntary shiver, and got in the Humvee. They dropped Richard at the helicopter site and raced back to the truck.

"What's going on?" Ava asked when he got into the driver's side of the truck.

"What do you mean?"

"You seem . . . creeped out," Ava said.

Seth started the truck and drove out of Piñon Canyon. They were a few miles down Highway 350 when he glanced at her.

"I have this feeling that something horrible happened there," Seth said.

"Where?"

"Bloom Ranch."

"We know they probably killed the tax agent," Ava said.

"More recently than that. What if . . ." Unwilling to give into the gloom, Seth shook his head. "What did his medical say?"

"Autoimmune disorder, they think," Ava said. "Of course, it's disability papers, so the information in that file is going to say autoimmune disorder brought on by exposure to toxins."

"The kind of toxins you might run into while playing Civil War?" Seth asked.

"Exactly," Ava said. "I bet we could get a warrant for his records at National Jewish."

"Why bother?"

"I think it's worth ruling out whether he's really sick."

"Why?"

"Because you have this creepy feeling that something horrible happened there," Ava said. "And they're using his illness to cover it up."

"Any idea what?"

"None. You?"

"The wife tried to leave him with the daughters, and he killed them all?" Seth shrugged.

"Maybe after he stole the bullets?" Ava asked.

"That's the only thing that comes to my mind. You?"

"Same. He must have buried them on the land," Ava said. "When did he start to get sick?"

"Principal said he was in the hospital last summer," Seth said. "Almost a year ago."

"We should check that," Ava said.

"Why?"

"Let's say he kills the wife and gets sick in August," Ava said. "That gives him a year for the bodies to decompose."

"That's why he's waiting until August," Seth said. "Makes sense."

"Didn't you find four unsolved shootings last summer?" Ava asked.

"Sure," Seth said. "Louisville, Tennessee. But

Gramps could have done those."

"Being in the hospital is his alibi for murder," Ava said. "So it could be either of them."

"Why would he need a cover?" Seth asked. "Doesn't seem like he's had one so far."

"What if he's holding them hostage?"

"They could be in counseling or something," Seth said.

"Counseling?" Ava asked.

"Or he could have killed them in October. How long does it take to dispose of a body?"

"For a high school science teacher?" Ava asked. "With Lye or Drano over the body and in this heat? Maybe a week on the outside. That would contaminate the ground water."

"Why wait until August?" Seth said.

"Because they're not dead yet." Ava gave an involuntary shiver. Clara lifted her head from the back seat to see if Ava needed her.

"You okay?" Seth asked.

Ava scooted over to sit next to him.

"Do you mind?" Ava asked.

Seth smiled, and she rested her head on his shoulder.

Twenty-one

They drove the rest of the way to Trinidad in silence. At the motel, they took Clara for a walk around the perimeter to shake off their gloom. When they returned to their room, Ava ducked into the bathroom. Clara jumped onto the bed, and Seth went to the desk where the yellow message light blinked.

"There's someone here for you," the motel manager said.

"Who?"

"Sheriff's deputy," the motel manager whispered. "Been waiting for you."

"We'll be right there," Seth said.

"Who is it?" Ava asked.

"Deputy sheriff," Seth checked his handgun and

put it back in the holster but didn't snap it in.

"Something going on?"

"No way to know," Seth said. "We've been stirring the pot in a small town. It's best to be prepared."

Ava nodded and put Clara in her crate. They went down the hall to meet the deputy sheriff. They stopped in the entryway to the breakfast area and lobby. From behind the counter, the manager pointed to a man sitting with his back to them.

"Sir," Seth said.

The deputy looked up. Seeing them, he stood. The deputy sheriff was tall and thickly built. He had the look of an aging quarterback and the large, light-gray felt Stetson of a southern Colorado rancher. He gave Ava a quick once-over before turning his full attention to Seth.

"You O'Malley?" the deputy asked.

"Seth O'Malley," Seth shook the deputy's hand.

"You must be Amelie Vivian Alvin," the deputy said. He didn't offer her his hand.

"I am," she smiled.

"I've followed your work," the deputy said. "Both of you. O'Malley, you're a legend. I drove the wife crazy with all the details of the Cigarette Killer. For the life of me, I didn't see that coming. And Saint Jude! Bastard who killed all those kids was a child psychiatrist?"

Uncomfortable, Seth looked around the room. Except for the motel manager, they were alone.

"And you!" The deputy turned to Ava. "You found the treatment for that First Responder's thing. Got an award from the president. You mind if I call you Ava?"

Ava shook her head.

"I'm Deputy Sheriff James Thatcher," he smiled. "Everybody who rides in the front calls me Jimmy. Those who ride in the back usually call me 'son-of-a-bitch.' But you'd know all about that."

He nodded to Seth and Seth smiled.

"Nice to meet you," Seth said. Ava shifted closer to Seth.

"It's a great honor to meet you," he said.

"What can we do for you?" Seth slipped his arm around Ava.

"We got a call from Denver PD that you were here," Jimmy said. "They asked if we would check out the science lab of Hoehne High School for a shooting up in Denver. Buddy of mine said you're looking into the Blooms."

His tone was neutral, but the deputy's posture indicated his intense interest.

"Do you know them?" Seth asked.

"Sure," Jimmy said. "My family and theirs, we've been in Piñon Valley for a century or more. I went to high school with Hill-three."

"Hill-three?" Seth asked.

"That's what we called him, 'Hill-three'. Lots of us have family names so we're all, Cody-four, or whatever. I'm just Jimmy."

"Why's that?" Seth asked.

"My family isn't so interested in pure blood lines and crap like that," Jimmy said. "My mom's from Michigan."

He gave Seth a big smile.

"Why are you looking into Hill-three?" Jimmy asked.

"We're wondering if he's up to something," Seth shrugged.

"Nah," Jimmy shook his head. "Magic O'Malley doesn't come all this way in the middle of the night to see if some high school science teacher is 'up to something.'"

Seth scowled at the deputy.

"We can always go into the office and talk," the deputy said.

Seth's expression didn't change. The deputy looked at Ava.

"Damn, I can't even last a couple of minutes under the famous O'Malley scowl," Jimmy beamed. "What do you want to know?"

"When was the last time you saw Bloom's wife?" Seth asked.

"Meldy?" the deputy looked surprised. "Meldy isn't around much."

"Marriage problems?" Ava asked.

"She works in Albuquerque at Sandia National Labs," Jimmy shrugged. "Only comes home on the weekends. Why?"

"She's been on leave from her job since early last summer," Seth said. "Family medical leave."

"Oh right, Hill-three's s'posed to be sick," Jimmy nodded.

"Supposed to be sick?" Ava asked.

"Oh, he had that thing when we were in high

school," Jimmy said.

"What thing?" Ava asked.

"I don't know what it is," Jimmy said. "Some kidney thing. Made him sick and sterile."

Jimmy nodded to Seth.

"Sterile?" Seth asked.

"Yeah," Jimmy gestured to the motel manager behind the counter. "Delores, isn't Hill-three sterile?"

"That's what he told everyone," the motel manager said. "I don't believe anything that man said. Ever."

"He used to brag about all the girls he bagged because he couldn't get 'em pregnant," Jimmy laughed.

The motel manager gave the deputy a disgusted look and went into the back.

"What about the kids?" Seth asked.

"They're not his," Jimmy said.

"Whose kids are they?" Ava asked.

"His brother's," Jimmy said. "Strangest thing. About ten years ago . . . no . . . I guess it's more like fourteen now, because my Dakota turned fourteen last week and their Ginny is the same age."

"What happened fourteen years ago?" Seth asked.

"Right," Jimmy said. "It was the damnedest thing, but Hill-three's brother was shot. They were living in Las Cruces and working at White Sands."

"They?"

"Howard – that's Hill-three's brother – and Meldy," Jimmy said. "It was a big deal because they never found out who killed him. They work on these hush-hush government projects, so they figured he was killed for what he knew, or whatever."

"Late nineties?" Seth asked.

"Yeah, that's right," Jimmy said. "How'd you know?"

"We're tracking unsolved murders around the country," Seth said. "There were a few of them in Las Cruces that year."

"You think Hill-three's a serial killer?"

"Murder-for-hire," Seth glanced at Jimmy to see what he thought of that.

"Sure, I bet you're right," Jimmy nodded. "I could see that. Probably to pay his taxes."

Jimmy's belly laugh echoed around the glass walls of the breakfast area. When Seth and Ava didn't respond, he stopped laughing.

"You're serious," Jimmy said.

Twenty-two

Seth nodded.

"Crap," Jimmy said. "His daddy too?"

"Just an idea," Seth shrugged. "You were telling us about Meldy Bloom. When did she marry Hill-three?"

"She was pregnant with Ginny when Howie died," Jimmy said. "Devastated. She's my cousin so she and the girls stayed with us for a while. We helped out as much as we could but . . . She wanted to sell her share of the ranch and get away, but . . ."

"Imelda Thatcher was my best friend in high school." The motel manager said as she walked toward them. "She and Howie started dating in junior high. His daddy didn't like it because the Thatchers aren't pure Piñon Valley like Jimmy told you. But Howie didn't care.

They went away to college together at Texas Tech. No one was surprised when they got married. When Howie died, she was destroyed. Her girls were just more than babies. There she was with a belly full of baby, and that Hillery wouldn't leave her alone. He was relentless, but you know why, right?"

"Why?" Seth asked.

"The Bloom land belonged to Howie's mother," Delores nodded. "When his momma died, she willed the land to the boys with the stipulation that their father could live out his life there. Two equal shares – the ranch land for Hill-three, and the hunting land around the Apishapa Wilderness Area for Howie."

"Hill-three loves to ranch," Jimmy said.

"There's more money in hunting," Delores said. "Showing tourists around and the like. It didn't surprise me when Hill-three ended up owning all of it. Didn't surprise me one bit."

"Why did she marry him?"

"She didn't know what else to do," Delores said. "He was sweet to her and the girls; said they were family, and on and on. She'd been with Howie so long that she'd basically grown up with Hill-three as an older brother. And he really turned on the charm. I'll tell you, she regretted it right after."

"How do you know?" Seth asked.

"She told me," Delores said. "She took the job in Albuquerque to get away from him. She and the girls would commute back and forth."

"She took the girls with her?" Seth asked.

"That's right," Jimmy nodded. "Until they wanted to stay here. My Melody and Ginny are close. The oldest, Hillary? She was a favorite of Hill-three's dad. She started going to school here when she was in junior high."

"They pumped the child up with stories of how their family were heroes in the Civil War," Delores said. "Meldy was horrified, but there wasn't much she could do about it."

"Did the other girls go to school here?" Seth asked.

"Not until high school," Jimmy said. Delores nodded.

"When was the last time you saw Meldy?" Seth asked.

Jimmy and Delores looked at each other and shrugged.

"The girls?" Ava asked.

"I saw them at graduation," Jimmy said. "All of them were there when Hillary, the oldest, graduated."

"And their mom?" Seth asked.

"Hill-three said she was doing some testing or something secret for the government," Jimmy shook his head. "I thought it was weird. I mean, Meldy loved those girls but . . . Did you see her?"

Her eyes filled with worry, and Delores bit her lip and shook her head. Seth sensed that she wasn't telling him everything.

"Anything you want to add?" Seth asked.

"If there's anything," Ava said. "Every detail helps us figure out what's going on."

Delores glanced at Jimmy.

"I'm not gonna tell anyone anything, Del," Jimmy said. "You know I won't."

"She used to come here with a man from work," Delores said.

"A man?"

"She said that she and Hill-three were getting divorced," Delores said. "She was waiting for the divorce to be final, and Hillary to graduate high school. I saw them in the pool . . . uh . . . the two younger girls and her guy. They were having a great time. They seemed really, really happy. And Meldy, for the first time since Howie died, she actually seemed at ease."

"When was that?" Seth asked.

"I'd have to look," Delores said. "Sometime last year."

"Last summer?" Seth asked.

"No. Meldy, the younger girls, and her guy spent most of the summer on an island off Vancouver," Delores said.

"She's on family medical leave from Sandia," Seth said. "While her husband was in the hospital."

"Who'd you hear that from?" Jimmy asked.

"Hoehne principal, I guess," Seth said.

"He must be going for disability," Jimmy said.

"Of course he is," Delores said. "You know how he lies!"

"He can spin a yarn," Jimmy nodded. "I pulled over Hill-three, his dad, and Hillary on their way out of town in . . . uh . . . July, maybe. They were going to Gettysburg again."

"Pulled them over?" Seth asked.

"Speeding," Jimmy said. "The girl, Hillary, was driving. Even so, I wrote 'em a ticket."

"So, there's a record," Seth said.

"Should be," Jimmy said.

"I'm having a hard time getting a handle on how sick the man is," Seth said. "It's all a little cockeyed."

"How so?" Jimmy asked.

"The principal indicated Mr. Bloom was quite ill. The U.S. Army deputy counsel general says he was healthy as a horse. Now you're saying he couldn't have been in the hospital, because he was in Gettysburg."

"Sure," Jimmy nodded.

"Sure?" Seth raised his eyebrows in surprise.

"Hill-three only has to stop taking his pills for a couple or four days and he gets real sick," Jimmy said. "Take the pills a few days, and he's better. If he's in the hospital, it'll show up in his blood, so they keep him a while."

"You know this because . . ."

"He did it a few times in high school," Jimmy said. "To get out of stuff he didn't want to do."

"Delores. Jimmy," Ava gave them a bright smile. "You can see how confused we are. You know these people. We don't. What do you think is going on here?"

"Did you say something about the Army?" Jimmy glanced at Ava as if to say, 'I'll get there.' "Hill-three sold out?"

"Deal's final in August," Seth said.

"Meldy must be dead," Delores said.

"Why?" Seth asked.

"Howie's buried on the edge of the Wilderness Area in their favorite spot," Delores said. "New man or no, she'd never let the Army have the land. Ever."

"She's right," Jimmy said. "And I'd have to say that I don't know what's going on. Honestly, I always thought Hill-three had a screw loose, and you can see how Delores feels."

"Will you go out to take a look?" Seth asked.

"Sure as shit. This is definitely probable cause for a look-see," Jimmy said. "I'll gather up a few guys. You want to come?"

Seth looked at Ava, and she nodded.

"We'll be there."

"I'd better go with you," Delores said. "My pa used to work for the Blooms. I spent my summers there."

"Does your dad work there now?" Seth asked.

"No. They stopped hiring in, maybe ten years ago," Delores said. "Said the business had changed, and they didn't need the help."

"One more thing," Seth said. "Have you seen Hill-three lately?"

"At graduation, like I said," Jimmy said. "Have you Del?"

Delores shook her head.

"It's not unusual," Jimmy said. "They live way out in the valley. We live in town."

"We don't try that hard to see them either," Delores said. "At least I don't."

"Thank you," Seth held his hand out for Delores, and she shook it. Turning to Jimmy, he asked, "You'll let us know?"

Delores went behind the counter to make calls for backup.

"I'll get the dogs," Jimmy said. "Give me twenty minutes then come down to the office. Del, you'll meet us there?"

Delores looked up from the telephone and nodded. Jimmy winked at Ava and left the hotel. Seth and Ava walked arm in arm to their room.

"Well, what do you think?" Ava asked. She bent to let Clara out of her crate.

"What do you think?" Seth asked.

"I think . . ." Ava looked at him and smiled. "I think you should take me to a really expensive dinner, fill me with expensive wine, and then take advantage of me."

Seth smiled at her but didn't respond.

"Ok," Ava said. "I don't think this is very complicated. Guy shoots people. Guy shoots brother and marries brother's wife to get the land. It's like something out of a Greek tragedy or Shakespeare or both."

"And the wife? Meldy? Where is she?"

"I don't know."

"Any sense of it?"

"No," Ava said. "While they were talking, I wondered if she was hiding out someplace."

"Not a hostage or a prisoner?"

"Just hiding out until the time is right," Ava nodded.

"I hope so," Seth said. "I can't figure out why he needs the money now. I mean, he took the rich contract in

Denver. He's selling this land that's been in his family forever. Why now?"

"Because the wife is divorcing him?" Ava asked.

"What do you mean?" Seth asked.

"How about this?" Ava smiled. "He takes the rich contract to pay the wife for the land in the divorce proceedings. Something happens. Maybe he realizes she had someone else or whatever . . ."

"He kills her and has to get rid of the land," Seth said. "Could be. I think we're missing something."

"Why?"

"We have unanswered questions," Seth said. "We know you, your father, your sisters and your mother are on the hit list. The two marshals make seven, right?"

"Who's the eighth hit?" Ava nodded.

"And why now?" Seth asked. "I know I keep asking the same question, but it feels crucial. And why finalize the deal in August? Hunting season starts in August and ends around December down here. He's missing out on taking all that money from all those rich Texans. Unless . . ."

"Unless what?"

"Unless selling in some way saves the land," Seth said.

"What do you mean?"

"Remember, Richard said he thought Bloom would screw them out of the land?" Seth asked. "What if he sold it now because he knew the Army couldn't use it? He'd get to keep the land, title free, and this Army nuisance would be gone."

"Could be," Ava said.

"What does pretending to be sick get him?" Seth asked.

"Alibis," Ava said. "He was in the hospital when . . . when . . . You're right, we're missing something."

Seth nodded. She smiled at him and sat down on the bed.

"You up for this thing?" Seth asked. "I can always go alone."

"I want to go," Ava said. "I want to find Meldy and those girls."

"You sure?"

"I can't just sit around waiting for someone to shoot me, Seth," Ava said. "I want to find them first. Plus, I bet this backwater could use a good forensics tech."

Seth smiled.

"That would be me," she smiled.

"A great forensics tech," he said. "I thought you had a job at the DPD."

"Haven't signed on the dotted line," she said. "Maybe they'll make me a better offer."

He nodded, and she laughed.

"Come on," Ava said. "Let's go see a man about a horse."

"What horse?"

"That's what you say in the country when you've got something important to do," Ava smiled. "You don't know because you're a big-city detective Hollywood music type."

"I see," Seth said. "A horse . . . and a murder and some ranch land."

"Exactly," she nodded.

"And expensive dinner?"

"Let's order in pizza and snuggle," she said.

"Murder first, snuggle later."

"And pizza."

"And pizza," he repeated.

"What do you think of that?"

"I do like horses," he said.

"I know," she said.

|-||-|||-||-|||-||-|||-||-|||-||-|||-||-|||-||-|||

Twenty-three

"It's O'Malley," Seth said into his cell phone. "Where are you?"

"At the fort," Richard Sarkasian, the U.S. Army deputy counsel general said.

"You'd better get here," Seth said.

"Where's here?"

"Bloom Ranch, southern parcel, near the house," Seth said. "I'm here with the Las Animas sheriffs."

"What did you find?"

"You should just come," Seth said.

"What did you find?" he repeated.

"You won't believe me if I tell you," Seth said.

"Try me."

"Let's just say that you were right in saying that by

selling the land, he was saving the land," Seth said. "I think you'll find it unusable in the near future."

"How did he do it?"

"Fracking," Seth said.

"Jesus fu . . ." The call abruptly ended.

Seth turned around to look at the scene unfolding behind him. Deputy Sheriff Jimmy Thatcher led six other deputies in full body armor and gas masks into the metal barn. Called "fracking," the process involved injecting highly pressurized fluid into the deep rock layer thus releasing natural gas. In the best of times, with the best intentions and the best, most careful technicians, fracking could be an environmental disaster.

The Blooms were neither experts nor had the best intentions. They had managed to both contaminate the ground water and to release a quantity of methane that required the sheriff's deputies to wear gas masks. For all intents and purposes, this portion of Bloom ranch would be unusable for the U.S. Army for the foreseeable future.

Seth smiled when he saw Ava. When they arrived, she had taken charge of two sheriff's deputies. They had gone through the Bloom residence looking for evidence of Meldy or the girls. Walking toward him, she shook her head.

"Nothing?" he asked.

"Not a hair or toy or scrap of clothing," Ava said. "Everything seems almost too clean – museum clean. I doubt anyone has lived here in . . . years, ten or twenty years maybe. Just kept it clean."

"Then where are they?" Seth asked.

"You saw . . ." Ava pointed to the back of the house. A few Sheriffs were carefully raking large vegetable beds where the dogs had indicated human remains might be buried. "Did they find . . .?"

A deputy in the garden whistled and waved. Seth and Ava jogged to the garden bed. Ava dropped to her knees beside the small trench.

"What is it?" Seth asked.

The sheriff's deputy had uncovered three small clumps of what looked like fat and tissue.

"Human remains?" the deputy asked.

"Possibly," Ava said. "They've been butchered – maybe ground or chopped up. It looks like he expected them to decompose."

"Good bet," the deputy said.

"Another month and we'd never have found this," Ava said.

Ava held up her hand, and Seth gave her a pair of gloves. While they watched, she used her fingertips to go through the clumps of dirt and tissue.

"Knew it!" Ava said. She pulled out a tiny finger bone. "These always get left behind."

"Human?" the deputy asked.

"Fifth intermediate and distal phalanges from a good-sized hand," Ava said. "I bet we can get DNA from the marrow."

"Is it Meldy or the kids?" Horrified, the deputy looked every day of his fifty some years.

"I'd say it's an adult – probably male by the thickness," Ava said as she stood up. She turned to the deputy. "Can you do something for me?"

"Yes ma'am," the deputy said.

"Can you guard this?" Ava asked. "We need to call in the Colorado Bureau."

"The CBI? Them boys are a pain in the assets."

Seth nodded.

"They are," Ava smiled. "But there's no way we can do the kind of job they can do in this garden. They're the State's forensic experts. We need them, or Bloom will go free."

"Plus, we need to find those children," Seth said.

"You sure they aren't in one of these beds?" the deputy asked.

"No, I'm not sure," Seth said.

"But?"

"He's having a Magic O'Malley moment," Ava said.

"You Magic O'Malley?" the deputy asked. Rather than protest, Seth smiled. "I didn't realize. Okay, I'll stay right here. In fact . . ."

The deputy whistled, and the deputy sheriffs in the garden area turned to look at him.

"We need to stop digging," the deputy said. "You, Tommy. Get the tape. We're goin' to tape this off. Jerry, call the CBI."

"Forensics. In Pueblo," Ava said.

"Ah, man, those boys is a pain in the rear," Jerry the deputy said.

"Even if they are, Magic O'Malley says we need them here," Deputy Robinson said.

The other deputies turned to look at Seth.

"When you're done, I could use some help finding Mrs. Bloom and her kids," Seth said.

The deputies jumped into action.

"You sure you can find them?" Ava asked.

"I hope so," Seth said.

A car door slammed and Delores the motel manager rushed to the garden.

"Is that her? Is that Meldy?" Delores's voice cracked with hysteria.

Before Seth could stop her, Delores dropped down to the garden. Her hand stretched out in horror toward the tissue. Seth pulled her up and held her to him.

"Ma'am," Ava said. "We don't know who it is at this time."

"They think it's a man, Del," Deputy Robinson said.

When she was steady, Seth released Delores. She went back to the bed, bowed her head in prayer, and then turned back to Seth.

"What can I do?" Delores asked.

"We're getting together a party to find Mrs. Bloom and the kids," Seth said.

"They aren't here somewhere?" Delores looked around the homestead.

"No," Seth said. "Would you mind going with Ava to look at the house?"

"Sure," Delores said. "What's going on here?"

"We're hoping you might be able to help with that," Seth said.

"Where do you think Meldy is?" Delores asked.

"Somewhere over there," Seth pointed to the northwest of where they were standing.

"On the state wilderness land?" Deputy Robinson's eyebrows shot up with surprise. "There's eight thousand acres there. That's a needle in a haystack."

"On the Wilderness land?" Delores turned to look at Seth.

"If that's over there," Seth said.

"I've been somewhere . . ." Delores's voice faded. "It's been years . . ."

"Del dated Hill-three in high school," the deputy said.

Surprised, Seth and Ava turned to Delores.

"I was young and stupid," Delores said.

"She married up," Deputy Robinson smiled.

"Have you met my husband?" Delores laughed and gestured to the deputy.

Ava and Seth smiled at them. Deputy Robinson laughed and leaned on his rake, and then remembered that he was standing over a body. He scowled.

"You've been somewhere?" Seth asked.

"They have a kind of hunting blind near the Wilderness Area," Delores nodded. "Howie built it when we were in high school. He used to take Texans hunting. He made good money doing it."

"Do you think you can find it?" Seth asked.

"Maybe, but . . ." Delores shook her head.

"But?" Ava moved closer to Delores.

"My dad used to stock it with beer and stuff. Howie was too young to buy beer, but those good old boys love their Coors." Delores glanced at her husband. He shrugged. "At least I think . . ."

"Call him, Del," Deputy Robinson said. "I bet he'd be here in a heartbeat. He loves Meldy as much as we do."

Delores took out her cell phone and placed the call. While she waited for the call to connect, she noticed the activity in the barn.

"What's going on in there?" she asked.

"Fracking," Seth said.

"Fracking out of the Raton Basin. If I didn't see it with my own eyes, I'd never . . ." Delores shook her head. Her father must have answered, because she turned away to talk on the phone.

"Listen," Seth said to Deputy Robinson. "Have you seen Hillery the third lately?"

Twenty-four

"I rarely see the man," Deputy Robinson said. "And never on purpose. You seen him lately, Jerry?"

"Nah," Jerry said. "Not since high school."

"How 'bout you Tommy?" Deputy Robinson caught the young man's arm as he walked by carrying yellow caution tape.

"What's the question?" the young deputy sheriff asked.

"Have you seen Hill-three lately?" Seth asked.

Tommy shook his head. Delores turned around. Her eyes glanced at Ava and then lingered on Seth, before she clicked off the phone.

"My dad's about fifteen minutes from here."

"Great," Seth said.

"They were fracking?" Delores asked.

"It would make the land unusable for the Army for a while," Seth said.

"At least five years," Ava said. "Maybe more."

"Figures," Delores said. "Where are all the people?"

"Good question," Deputy Robinson said. "There was no one here when we got here."

"It is strange," Seth said.

"You said something about looking at the house?" Delores said. "I don't know if I can help. I haven't been here in years."

"But you did spend time here?" Seth asked.

"Sure, before Hill-three's mom died, but that was twenty years or so ago," Delores said. "She used to invite me to stay for dinner if I was here."

"Let's take a look and see," Ava said. "You'd be surprised what someone who knows a house can notice."

Delores nodded and followed Ava to the house.

"What now?" Deputy Robinson asked.

"We wait," Seth said.

Seth took in all of the activity around him. The deputies were securing the fracking unit in the barn. Other deputies nudged him out of the way so that they could tape off the garden.

A few minutes later, a battered truck pulled up to the house. Seth walked over to meet Delores's father. He had stark white hair and the deeply lined skin of someone who'd spend most of his life working under the high desert sun. At least eighty, the man had the spry look and spring in his step of someone ready to get the job done. Seth glanced at the house and saw Ava waving to him from the upstairs balcony.

"O'Malley," Seth held his hand out, and the man shook it.

"Drew Gilpin," Delores's father said.

"Just Drew? Not Drew the second or third?" Seth smiled.

"Nah," Drew said. "Our family's on the working side of the equation in this valley. More names, less money."

"Good to meet you," Seth said.

"Nice to meet you, sir. I've read all about you and your investigations up in Denver. I didn't expect you to be such a young man."

Seth smiled.

"Do you really write music, too?" Drew asked. "Or is that just a part of the legend?"

"It's a gift and a curse," Seth said.

"I bet," Drew said. "Like that little gal up there."

Seth laughed out loud and Drew smirked.

"Del called and asked me to come over," Drew said. "I worked for one Hillery or another for most of my life. What can I help with?"

"I have an idea that Meldy Bloom and her kids are somewhere in that direction," Seth pointed to the northwest of where they stood. "Deputy Robinson suggested it was in the Wilderness Area."

"The Apishapa?" Drew nodded. "Makes some sense. You think he's holding them?"

"Maybe they're hiding from him and the oldest daughter," Seth said.

"Hillary?" Drew asked. "She's a sweetie. Why would Meldy hide out from her?"

Seth shrugged.

"I know she had a tough time at school, but underneath it all she's a real doll," Drew said. "Why, the last couple of years, she's spent her afternoons with my wife. Alice had MS and needed help taking care of the house. We pay her a little bit – not much. Hillary is a real help."

"Any idea where Hillary is now?" Seth kept his tone neutral.

"She said she had to go with her grandpa some place . . ." Drew shook his head. "Nope, I don't remember where. She has to drive because Hill-three has that kidney thing and can't drive. Her grandpa falls asleep at the wheel."

"The high school principal doesn't seem to like her much," Seth said.

"Sure. He's not from around here," Drew nodded. "He wouldn't cotton to a strong, bullheaded woman who doesn't necessarily abide by the rules. We raise 'em like that around here. Have you met my daughter?"

Drew laughed. Mid-laugh, he turned his head sideways and scowled at Seth.

"Why you askin' about Hillary?" Drew asked. "Is she in some kind of trouble?"

"I'm not sure," Seth said. "I'd like to find Mrs. Bloom and her kids. Maybe they'll have some idea what's going on."

"Where did you say you thought they were?" Drew asked.

"Delores suggested they might be at a hunting

blind?" Seth asked. "She said you used to stock it for Howard Bloom and his hunting guests."

"Oh sure," Drew nodded.

"Could you find it again?" Seth asked.

"How you going?" Drew asked.

"Horseback, I think," Seth said.

"Better to take a jeep. It's not far, but it's not close either."

"But you can find it,"

"Easy," Drew said. "You just go out old Houghton Road veer left at Dead man's Gulch, and turn left at Stringer. Go straight on past the Stringer windmill. Don't stop there, because you want the second one – Stringer two – near the stock pond. Probably green this time of year, but what would they expect when they get rid of all their experienced help. That boy Hill-three wouldn't know the right side of a Heifer if . . ."

"Where is the blind?" Seth cut off what was sure to be a well-practiced rant.

"Oh, right," Drew gave a guilty smile. "It's about a half mile from there. You could do that on horseback or foot."

Confused, Seth blinked at the man.

"That made more sense in my head," Drew laughed. "Let me get my map book."

Drew went to his truck and took out his *Colorado Atlas* topographic maps. He flipped through the pages until he came to the map page that included the Apishapa State Wilderness Area.

"This up here is all State Trust land," Drew said. "I

talked Howie into building the cabin just outside the Wilderness and Trust land."

"Cabin?"

"Blind; cabin," Drew shrugged. "It's a tiny place. I mean, he was a kid and look at me. I'm no expert carpenter. We built it in a month or so. He used the roof as a hunting blind. Hunters like to stay overnight – either camping out rustic or sleeping in the room – depending on the weather."

Seth leaned over the map.

"It's right here," Drew said. "Right outside Merrit Spring. You can get there by jeep. Easy. Horse'll just take longer. You're in a hurry?"

"I'm in a hurry," Seth said. "How . . ."

He glanced up at the horizon and turned back to the map.

"It looks a mess, but the roads're dry this time of year," Drew said. "You head out this way . . ."

Drew pointed toward the north.

"You'll run right into the old Houghton Road," Drew pointed to the road on the map. "It runs right into the Dead man's Gulch right by the old Houghton homestead. Did you check there?"

"Not yet," Seth said.

"I'm surprised Jimmy didn't go there first," Drew said.

"He's a little busy," Seth pointed to the barn where Deputy Sheriff Jimmy Thatcher was yelling over the noise at another deputy. Drew glanced where Seth pointed, and nodded.

"I doubt anyone's been there in . . . forty years,

probably longer," Drew said.

"We'll check it if we don't find them at the blind," Seth said.

"Anyway, I'd be happy to lead you out there," Drew said. "I bet Jimmy'd deputize me an' all."

Seth nodded.

"What are you drivin'?" Drew asked.

"I was thinking about taking that," Seth pointed into the sky. Drew looked up to see a military helicopter beginning to lower to the ground.

"You think they give a shit about anything?" Drew asked.

"No," Seth said. "But that won't stop me from asking for a ride."

Drew laughed. Out of the corner of his eye, Seth saw Ava and Delores leaving the Bloom residence. Seth raised an eyebrow to Drew and walked into the wash of the helicopter.

Twenty-five

He waited for a moment, and U.S. Army Deputy General Counsel Richard Sarkasian hopped out of the chopper. He glared at Seth and turned to look in the barn.

"Covered it in the metal barn," Richard said.

Seth nodded.

"We couldn't see it from the air or satellite," Richard said.

"Just looked like a steel barn," Seth said.

"Where is the bastard?" Richard asked.

"I think that's the question of the hour," Seth said. "No one seems to know. Last I heard, he was taking a driving trip."

Shaking his head, the lawyer glared at Seth.

"Listen, you're going to be here a while," Seth said.

"Right?"

Richard nodded.

"Mind if I borrow your ride?" Seth asked.

"Are you going to stick it to Hillery Bloom the third?" Richard asked.

"Something like that," Seth said.

"Then by all means," Richard said.

"Okay if I take a few deputies with me?" Seth asked.

"Leave me someone to tell me what's going on," Richard said.

Seth looked up to see Deputy Jimmy Thatcher walking toward them.

"There's your guy," Seth said.

"You know how to ride in one of those?" Richard asked.

Seth stared at the lawyer. The lawyer nodded.

"You're really going to make me say it," Seth said.

"Someone's got to say Mitch's lines," Richard smiled. "He's not here."

"I was easing my way in and out of helicopters and women while you were still hoping to lose your virginity, college boy."

Richard laughed. Seth smiled.

"One more thing," Seth said. "Know anyone in the press?"

"Why?" Richard asked.

"Hoping to flush your friend Hill-three out of wherever he's hiding," Seth said.

"I'll call. After . . ." Richard pointed to Jimmy.

Seth nodded and got into the helicopter to speak

with the crew. When he came out, Ava had organized the deputies. Deputy Robinson and the deputies he'd identified as Tommy and Jerry stepped past Seth into the helicopter. Ava, and Delores and her father got in next. Seth helped them strap in. Drew gave directions to the cockpit and came back to the passenger compartment. When Seth sat down, he put his headset on, and the helicopter took off.

Seth clicked the switch on his headset to the channel within the passenger compartment. He was fairly confident the sheriff's headsets were turned off.

"What did you find in the house?" Seth asked.

Hearing his voice, Ava turned to look at him. She moved her mouth, but he couldn't hear her. He pointed to the switch and she turned on her headset to speak with him.

"Hi beautiful," he smiled.

She reached over to hold his hand.

"What did you find in the house?" Seth asked.

"Not a lot more than we already knew," Ava said. "Delores agreed that it didn't look like they lived there. She said her mother told her Hill-three had an apartment in Hoehne that he used when he was teaching. Delores thought the girls lived with him in town during the school year. But . . . it's definitely weird. She said the house looked like a shrine to his mother."

"A shrine to a better time?" Seth asked.

"Probably," Ava said. "I wondered if it was a tax thing. I'd have to check, but I think you pay less property tax on a primary residence than a commercial property."

"Good point," Seth said. "If they weren't living out

here, this would be primarily a commercial operation."

"Right," Ava said. "The weirdest thing to Delores was the horses. The ranch has always bred amazing horses. I asked her about them being Arabian."

"Like the tax agent's horses?" Seth asked.

"Exactly," Ava said. "She said that people always said they looked like it, but . . ."

Ava shrugged.

"What, about the horses, was weird?" Seth asked.

"Meldy is a horse woman," Ava said. "She competes in long-distance races, like your librarian friend's daughter. Horses have always been a big part of the Bloom business. In fact, the horses are one of the reasons Meldy stayed married to Hill-three. She wanted to keep the horse business going."

"And?" Seth asked.

"Where are the horses?" Ava asked. "The barn is filled with fracking equipment. The corral is empty. Delores said the horses were always up here near the house."

"Boy, I don't know," Seth said. "I talked to Delores's dad about riding out to find the women. I was hoping to ride a mythical Piñon Canyon horse. It didn't occur to me that the horses weren't here."

"Did you see any horses?"

"I . . . No," Seth shook his head. "You're right. Where are the horses?"

Ava nodded.

"Did you get anything on our 'why-now' puzzle?" Seth asked.

"Nothing other than the bodies in the garden

beds," Ava shrugged.

Seth nodded.

"I know that look," Ava said. "What?"

"I'm thinking we should get the Denver coroner to do the autopsy on Hillery Bloom Jr."

"Hill-three's father? Why?"

"Just a hunch," Seth said.

Ava nodded.

"Mr. O'Malley?" the helicopter pilot broke into their conversation. "We're close to your destination. We can easily land near the stock pond … uh … Stringer windmill two."

"Stringer windmill two?" Seth asked. "Perfect."

"Would you like us to wait for you?" the pilot asked.

"We may have injured people," Seth said.

"You have state patrol choppers coming from Pueblo," the pilot said. "Press, too. We'll stay 'til they arrive."

"Thank you," Seth said.

The helicopter began to descend onto a nearly flat field of the upper Bloom ranch near the iridescent green stock pond. The helicopter blades whipped up a whirlwind of dust and sand on the dry field. When the helicopter was firmly on the ground, Seth slid open the door and hopped out. The deputy sheriffs, and Ava, Delores, and Drew followed.

"This way," Drew said.

Delores's father began walking at a fast clip down a dirt road. Seth and Ava started after him with the deputies following close behind. The road ended near the edge of a wash. They continued down the narrow wash until they reached a wide gully. They could see the wooden corner of the hunting blind. Seth whistled and Drew turned around. Seth waved him back.

"That's the cabin?" Seth asked.

"That's it," Drew said.

"We'll go on ahead," Deputy Robinson said. Out of breath, Delores arrived in the gully. "Del, you stay here in case there's something awful. You wanna go with us, O'Malley? You're not wearing body armor."

"You go ahead," Seth said. "Whistle once if we should join you, twice if we should bring Delores."

Twenty-six

Deputy Robinson nodded to Seth. He and the younger men checked their handguns. With a nod, the younger men started down the gully toward the spring. They were soon lost in the greener brush near Merrit spring. Deputy Robinson kissed his wife and followed the deputies down the gully.

They waited in tense silence. Seth tried to interpret every sound. The sudden boom was probably the deputies kicking in the door. There was a pop and then another – which could have been gunfire – but no screams, moans, or other sounds of human agony. After what seemed like an age, they saw the young deputy Tommy leaning over the top of the blind. He whistled once and then again.

Seth and Ava took off running. They found Deputy

Robinson coming back to get his wife. The deputy waited for Delores then trotted beside them.

"They were in there," Deputy Robinson said. "Tied up tight. The girls ... It's dreadful. I wanted to get Del, because..."

The deputy leaned to Seth.

"The little girls look like they've been assaulted. Meldy's been beaten pretty bad. When she saw me, she begged for Del. Do you mind?" Deputy Robinson glanced at Ava. "I know it's not police procedure but ..."

"Good idea," Seth said.

"We'll take a look when you have them out of there," Ava said.

"It's pretty bad, Del," Deputy Robinson said. "You sure you want to ..."

Delores's mouth formed a thin line as she started down the path. Deputy Robinson followed close behind. Drew started to go, but Seth grabbed his arm.

"There's nothing we can do," Seth said. "Let's give them some time. They're going to need their strength to get home and deal with what's next. What's next is always harder than what happened."

Drew grimaced and looked away from him.

"Why don't we see if we can get some emergency blankets from the helicopter?" Ava asked. "I bet they have water too. We can be right here when the deputies bring them out."

Drew nodded to Ava. Seth followed them out of the gully. They reached the road just in time to see the military helicopter take off. A Las Animas County sheriff's helicopter and a state patrol helicopter were landing nearby. Seth pointed Ava to the state patrol helicopter and went to explain the situation to the Las Animas county sheriff.

Drew grabbed a first aid kit and left to show the officers where to go. Seth and Ava stepped to the side to avoid getting in the way of the police officers as they went to and from the Merrit Spring cabin.

Hearing another helicopter, Seth looked overhead. News helicopters for Pueblo and Denver flew overhead. Just as they made their second pass with their camera men hanging out the door, Deputy Robinson and Delores, with Meldy between them, came onto the field. Seth and Ava ran to greet them. Meldy looked up into the cameras and then ran to the Las Animas county sheriff's helicopter.

State patrolmen carried her daughters on stretchers onto the field. Seth and Ava helped to hide the children's faces from the cameras. They made their way across the field and into the Sheriff's helicopter. With the children safe, Ava nodded to Seth and ran to the cabin. Seth stepped into the helicopter.

"I'll give you two minutes while I strap them in," the medic said.

Seth nodded. He introduced himself to Meldy Bloom.

"What happened?" Seth asked.

"Hill went nuts," Meldy said. "Everything was fine, really fine. Out of nowhere, he went bonkers. He killed Phillip and his brother and . . ."

"Any idea why?" Seth asked.

"No idea," Meldy said. "We were going to live in

Albuquerque. He just . . . He started fracking and ranting and beating on me, saying I destroyed everything and . . ."

Meldy started to cry.

"We can talk later," Seth said.

"No," Meldy said. "You have to find my daughter, Hillary. He's making her do awful things. He said he would kill us if she didn't do exactly what he told her to do. And . . . you have to find my husband. He told these girls he would kill me and . . ."

"Ok, that's enough," the medic said.

Seth nodded. He was about to leave, when Meldy grabbed his arm.

"Find my husband, Detective O'Malley. Find my daughter," Meldy said. "You found all those other people and killers. Find them. She's just a girl and he. . . "

"Go." The medic used his body to push Seth away from Meldy.

The helicopter engine began to rev and Seth jumped out. The sheriff's helicopter rose over the field. Meldy, her daughters, and Delores were on their way to the Level I Trauma Center hospital in Denver.

"You coulda gone with them," Deputy Robinson said.

"We're on a different journey," Seth said. "I'm glad they're safe."

"What'd she say?" Deputy Robinson asked.

"Find her daughter," Seth shrugged.

Deputy Robinson gave a worried look after the helicopter and left to return to the cabin. Seth took out his cell phone and called Captain Ferguson.

"Hey Ferg," Seth said.

"What?" Ferg's voice betrayed the irritation of long nights and frustrated days.

"Where's the attitude coming from?" Seth laughed.

"Just that feeling that I'm not going to like what you want me to do," Ferg said.

"You know about Meldy Bloom and the kids?" Seth asked.

"They're on their way here," Ferg said. "That's what I know."

"Mrs. Bloom is worried about her daughter," Seth said. "Said her husband told her he would kill her mother and sisters if she didn't do what he wanted."

"So you're thinking . . ."

"The eighth victim is Yvonne Smith," Seth said.

"So you're thinking . . ." Ferg repeated.

"The girl's at the airport," Seth said.

"On it," Ferg hung up the phone.

Standing in the middle of the field, Seth tried to make sense of everything. Before coming to southern Colorado, he'd thought the Blooms ran a tidy little murder-for-hire business to pay their property taxes. Moving away from the helicopters, he found a quiet patch of sand not far from the stock pond. He broke off a dry mesquite branch and wrote a timeline in the sand:

BLOOM MOTHER DIES

– SPLITS UP THE RANCH

HOWIE B IS KILLED BY HILL3

MELDY B MARRIES HILL3

- UNHAPPY

MB WORKS AT SANDIA NTNL LABS

- COMMUTES

MB ASKS FOR DIVORCE

MB TAKES LEAVE FROM JOB

- VACATIONS WITH KIDS

H&H TAKE LARGE CONTRACT

- 8 LIVES TO BUY LAND FROM M

Those facts took him to last fall. What the hell happened last fall to make Hill-three go, according to his wife, "bonkers"?

"You think they killed their mom?"

Seth turned to find Deputy Jimmy Thatcher standing just behind him.

"Do you?" Seth asked.

"Could be," Jimmy said. "She was shot. Happened on their range. It was s'posed to've been an accident. No one was charged."

"Any idea who did the shooting?" Seth asked.

"Uh . . ." Jimmy looked down at the sand before nodding his head. "I'd have to check. I bet the sheriff would know right off, but I think it was her husband, Hill-three's dad. But he's the kind of guy who'd, you know, take the blame."

"I guess I'm just wondering what happened last fall," Seth said.

"What do you mean?" Jimmy asked.

"I had a chance to speak with Mrs. Bloom before she left for Denver," Seth said. "She said that Hill-three went bonkers, crazy."

"I told you, he was always like that," Jimmy said. "You sure Hill-three is a murderer?"

"Pretty sure. Why?"

"He could never stand the sight of blood," Jimmy said. "It was a big deal at the school. They never dissected anything that bled. My Bethany wants to be a doctor, so she asked if they could dissect a mammal. I caught a rabbit for the class to dissect. Hill-three took one look at the poor bleeding bunny and fainted. He . . ."

Seth looked at the ground and then stared at Jimmy.

"You're creeping me out, O'Malley," Jimmy said. "What did I say?"

"You solved the whole thing," Seth said. "Thanks. Now, how do we get out of here?"

"You can take my jeep," Jimmy said. "But we've got plenty of work to do. You wouldn't want to maybe volunteer to help. Sheriff sent me over here to ask. We could sure use the help."

"I bet if we stand here a few more minutes, we'll hear from the CBI," Seth said.

"They took over at the house and . . ."

Four SUV's pulled up with "Colorado Bureau of Investigation" on the door.

"Shit," Jimmy said. "How'd you know?"

"I've done this a while," Seth said.

"Come on," Jimmy said. "Let's talk to the jerks and get out of here. If this's been on the tube, my wife's gonna wanna know I'm all right."

Seth used his boot to wipe out his list in the dirt and went to find Ava. He followed the stream of CBI agents down to the cabin and stood silent guard until she appeared. She was deep in conversation with a CBI forensics colleague when she saw him. She smiled at him and happily turned the scene over to the CBI. Soon, they were sitting in the back of Jimmy's tightly packed SUV. She slipped her small hand between his knees, and he put his arm around her.

"Hey, none of that," Jimmy said when Seth leaned in to kiss Ava. Seth laughed and kissed her anyway. "You guys want to come back to my house for a barbeque. The rest of these guys are coming."

"Nah," Seth said. "We need to save our puppy from her crate."

"Save the puppy from her crate," Jimmy and the other deputies laughed. "That's a new one. I've never heard it called that."

Ava blushed and the deputies laughed. The

conversation turned to the upcoming barbeque mixed with their hatred of the CBI, and Ava rested against Seth.

"You seem calmer," Ava said in his ear. "Did you figure it out?"

"I think so," Seth said.

"I love that about you," Ava said.

She leaned into him, and they rode the rest of the way back to the house in quiet closeness.

|-||-|||-||-|||-||-|||-||-|||-||-|||-||-|||-||-|||

Twenty-seven

Seth felt a growing pain somewhere in the back of his brain. Not prone to headaches, he was certain the loud man standing in front of him was the source of his pain. Seth glanced at his watch. The CBI agent in charge hadn't stopped talking for more than fifteen minutes. He kept saying he wanted to make sure he and Seth were "simpatico" and "in alignment," but he hadn't stopped talking long enough for Seth to speak.

"So what do you think?" the agent-in-charge asked.

Surprised the man's sudden silence, Seth managed a nod.

"We're on the right track," the agent-in-charge said. "I *knew* it."

The agent-in-charge walked away.

"Hey guys!" the agent-in-charge yelled as he walked toward the metal barn. "Magic O'Malley thinks we're on the right track."

Seth rubbed his head with his hand.

"Nice of you," Ava laughed.

Seth scowled at her and continued rubbing his head. The agent-in-charge called Ava to him. She winked at Seth and ran off. Seth turned around to see if he could find some water. He was halfway to the water station when his cell phone rang.

"O'Malley."

"You sumunabitch," a man's voice said. "You almost got me shot."

Seth took the phone away from his ear to look at it.

"Sheriff Elliot," Seth said. "How are you?"

"Alive, no thanks to you," Sheriff Jeb Elliot said. "What the hell are you doing giving a woman a loaded gun?"

"Sexist?"

"This woman! This woman!" The mock hostility in Jeb's voice shifted to laugher. "Ah hell, Seth. Viv almost shot me."

"I seem to remember something about hand grenades and horseshoes."

Jeb laughed.

"What happened?" Seth asked.

"That sumunabitch murderer was here, right here, in her hotel," Jeb said. "Sitting in the waiting area watching the TV. I came to pick up Viv and her O'Malley-approved chastity escort, Janet, for dinner. I'm walkin' in when Viv sees the sumunabitch, yells, and pulls out a handgun. 'Course the gun goes off while she's pulling it from her pocket. Viv starts screaming and waving the gun. Chastity expert Janet gets the gun away from her to shoot him, and he's gone."

"What do you mean gone?" Seth asked.

"Gone," Jeb said. "Disappeared. Evaporated. I was so distracted by trying not to get shot that I didn't see him go. Guy at the desk said he took one look at Viv, got up, and walked out the door."

"Did anyone see him outside?" Seth asked.

"You know, O'Malley," Jeb said. "They gave me this shiny, pointed star because it goes with my hat."

Seth chuckled.

"Our guys canvassed the area and no one saw nothing," Jeb said.

"Security tape?" Seth asked.

"Same thing," Jeb said. "He's watching the TV. Looks up when Viv shouts 'Hey!' and he walks out before Viv shoots at me."

"Any idea what he was watching?" Seth asked.

"Now how did I know you were going to ask me that?" Jeb asked.

"You're the sheriff?"

"Oh yes, that's right. I am the sheriff. Let's see, that sumunabitch was watching the release of captives in southern Colorado," Jeb said. "You can see it on the security tape. He sees a helo shot of the lady running next to a Las Animas sheriff. Hillery Bloom the third, aka the sumunabitch, stands up and walks out. I assume that's your work."

"I'm standing in the southern Colorado Desert working to solve *your* cold cases," Seth said.

"Mighty nice of you," Jeb said. "Now, if you don't mind, I'm taking Viv back to my ranch. Janet's coming too, in case you're worried. I hired her as my personal assistant. I've needed one for a while, and retirement doesn't suit her much."

"Uh," Seth said.

"I'm going to say this one time, so you'd better listen up," Jeb said. "My Patty and Vivian were best friends in high school. When my Patty got real sick, she told me that she and Viv had both liked me in high school; the girls made a bet as to who I'd take out first. I always knew me a snake in the grass, and that Alvin practically slithered to the altar, but Viv . . . She's not too smart about people."

"She trusts you," Seth said.

"I'd say the same for you, but we already determined that you're a sumunabitch," Jeb said. "Anyway, Patty made me promise that, after she was gone, of course, if I ever had the chance, I should try to make a life with Viv. Your email came on the five-year anniversary of her death. I thought it was my Patty nagging me from the great beyond. You remember what she could be like."

"I do."

"So, I came myself to see what was what."

"I'm sorry," Seth said.

"Nope," Jeb said. "You were doing what you should. I just want you to know that if I can swing it, I'm gonna be your father-in-law, sooner rather than later."

Jeb snorted a laugh and hung up. Seth smirked and walked to the water station. It had been a long, hot day. He was looking forward to a shower, a meal, and having Ava all to himself. He nodded to the deputy standing at the water station. Seth picked up a blue plastic cup and then looked at the big orange thermal water jug.

"Any idea where this water came from?" Seth asked.

"That well over there," the deputy said. "Worried?"

"I thought they contaminated the groundwater here," Seth said.

"They have a fancy filter system here," the deputy said. "It was a big deal to Mrs. B, Hill-three and Howie's mom. She thought it might help Hill-three with his illness. Plus, Hill-three's daddy had some trouble with his water growing up. I don't know what, but it was a big deal to Mrs. B to get the system installed. I don't think it'll hold out for long, but we were able to get clean water today. That douche from the Army said they tested the well. It was a condition of the sale. The CBI tested it when they came today. It's clean."

"You remember what was wrong with Mr. Bloom's water?" Seth asked.

"Lead, I think," the deputy said.

"How . . .?"

"I was good friends with Howie, sir," the deputy said. "I used to hunt with him, fish and camp – stuff boys do here in southern Colorado. He was a good guy. I was real sorry when he died."

"Do you know Meldy, too?"

"Not much," the deputy said. "She was Howie's

girl. That's about it. They moved away right after high school, but we always got together when he was in town."

"Thank you," Seth said. "One more question."

"Shoot."

"You wouldn't happen to know how long it takes to get from here to Rapid City would you?" Seth asked.

"No, but I can check on my phone." The deputy took a smartphone from his pocket and started pressing the buttons. "Looks like nine hours by car. You think you'd go by car?"

"Probably. You?"

"I would," the deputy said. "Planes are damned expensive and you'd have to rent a car wherever you went. You going to South Dakota?"

"Just curious," Seth smiled. "Thanks for your help."

"You bet," the deputy said. "Try the water. You'll like it."

Seth filled his cup with water, smelled it, and took a drink. It tasted cold and clean. He took a long drink and refilled his glass. His headache was starting to ease.

Little by little, McGinty's old bone was falling into place. He checked his watch. He calculated the time since Meldy was rescued. At the very minimum, he had six hours before he had to worry about Hill-three showing up for Ava. From the barn area, she looked up at him. He gestured her over.

"What's up?" she asked.

"Let's get out of here," Seth said.

"You don't have to ask me twice," Ava laughed. "You don't want to check in before we go?"

"I don't," Seth said.

Laughing, she followed him to his truck, and they were on their way back to the hotel.

"Pizza and cuddle?" Seth asked.

"Mmm, I was thinking shower, cuddle, pizza," Ava said. "You?"

"Sounds good to me," Seth said.

Ava turned up the air conditioning, and they drove along Highway 160 in companionable silence. They were almost to Highway 350 when Ava turned down the air conditioning.

"Seth?" Ava turned to look at him.

"I know," he said.

"I know you know," Ava said. "I'd still like to say it anyway."

"Sounds fair," Seth said.

"I feel like I don't know who I am anymore," Ava said. "A year ago, my father was the Colorado state attorney and I ran the best damned backup forensics lab in the state. Now, he's dead and I . . . Everything I thought was true about my life, my family's life, me . . . Everything was a big, fat lie."

He glanced at her to see if she was crying. She was too lost in thought and strong emotion to cry.

"I want to be with you," Ava said. "I want to marry you, to spend my life with you, but I have to know me first. I can't jump from daughter of Colorado State Attorney to daughter of a pandering jerk to Mrs. O'Malley."

"What's changed?" Seth asked. "When everything happened with your father, you didn't . . ."

"I've changed, I guess," Ava said. "I see how *weak* my mother is, and Bella. . ."

Ava began to cry.

"I have to know who I am, where I belong on the planet, before I can be your wife," Ava's voice cracked with sorrow. "I don't want to lose you, lose us, but I look inside, and I can't find me. I have to be me before I can be us."

"I understand," Seth said.

"That's what I hate about you," Ava said. "You understand. You want what's best for me. You want me to be whole."

"And that's bad?"

"You'll just continue on," Ava said. "I'll leave, you'll sleep for a day or so and then you'll play the piano. You'll finish the piece you started, do the hard work, and sell it. When I come back, you'll be solving mysteries and playing the piano. You're so . . . you."

Not really sure what she meant, Seth nodded.

"I want that," Ava said.

"Not everyone is like me, Ava," Seth said. "Mitch wasn't. Maresol isn't. Dale will never be. My brothers sure weren't."

"Sandy is," Ava said.

"She got that way by going through hell," Seth said. "My other two daughters, Lizzy and Julie Ann, aren't like me. Lizzy can't decide what to wear most days, and Julie Ann is . . . well, a good Marine. The way I am; it's not really . . ."

"Normal," Ava said.

"Valuable," Seth said.

"It's valuable to me," Ava said.

Seth nodded.

"I've hurt you," Ava stated the obvious.

"I understand," Seth said.

Ava turned her tear-stained face away from him to look out at the barren desert landscape. He pulled into the parking lot of the hotel.

"Have I hurt you?" Ava asked.

"The situation hurts," Seth said. "I understand how you feel, but to me, you're the same woman I met. You're the same woman I held while you sobbed in the shower when Beth was killed. You're the same woman who came to live with me after your father sold your condo. You're the same woman who screamed and threw things when your father was arrested and sold out your mother and sisters. And now, you're the same woman experiencing deep grief over the loss of her sister. To me, you haven't changed, but I understand you feel different to you. I know what that feels like."

Ava leaned toward him. Her hand stroked his cheek, and she kissed him.

"And I think you're wrong," Seth said.

"Wrong?"

"You are like me – you're calm and directed in the middle of the storm. According to your mother, Dale, your sisters, you've been that way your entire life. It's who you are. I get that you don't feel stable right now, but that doesn't mean that you aren't. Mostly, I think you're exhausted."

Thinking about what he said, Ava stared at him.

"One thing that is constant is that I love you," Ava said. "That's what confuses me the most. How can I still love you so much and. . . all of this?"

"Maybe because we find our true selves through our love for each other," Seth said.

Ava gave him a puzzled look.

"Come on," Seth said. "Let's rescue our puppy, clean up, and get some pizza."

"And cuddle?"

"Are you up for that?" Seth asked.

"I'm confused, O'Malley, not dead," Ava laughed and got out of the truck.

Shaking his head, he followed her into the hotel.

|-||-|||-||-|||-||-|||-||-|||-||-|||-||-|||-||-|||

Twenty-eight

"Seth?" Ava said when she opened the door to the bathroom where he was showering. "Captain Ferguson is on the phone."

"What's he want?" Seth asked.

"He won't tell me," Ava said. "I'm going to take Clara out while you and your boyfriend discuss your business. I ordered the pizza."

Seth nodded his thanks.

"Are you coming out?" Ava asked.

"I'm not sure," Seth said.

"Tell you what," Ava said. "I'll leave the phone right here."

She leaned in to give him a stirring kiss and left the bathroom. He waited a minute for his pulse to even, before getting out to talk to Captain Ferguson.

"O'Malley."

"It's about blooming time," Ferg said.

Seth laughed. He wrapped a towel around his waist and went into the room to find his clothes.

"I hope I'm interrupting something good," Ferg said. "You naked?"

"I just got out of the shower. So, yes."

"And Ava?"

"She left with the dog," Seth said.

"Naked?" Ferg laughed.

"You sound chipper," Seth said.

"I sent Harry to the airport to follow up on your lead," Ferg said. "I thought some good-looking bait might catch us a young lady killer."

"What did handsome Harry catch on his fishing trip?"

"A killer," Ferg said. "Well . . ."

"What happened?"

"We found her on the manifest for a flight from DIA to Los Angeles," Ferg said.

"Going after Yvonne," Seth said.

"And she knew where Yvonne was," Ferg said. "I didn't know where Yvonne was – no one here knew where she was, how . . .?"

"Whoever hired the Blooms has access to a lot of secure information," Seth said. "The son, Hillery Bloom the third, came after Vivian today."

"In Rapid City?"

"Yep," Seth said.

"Someone has contacts," Ferg said. "I swear it's not . . ."

"Never occurred to me."

"It better not," Ferg said.

"What happened with Harry?" Seth found his underwear in a ball near the bed. Holding the phone between his shoulder and ear, he pulled them on.

"Right," Ferg said. "I sent Harry to DIA. He used his badge to get on the terminal. He found her right away in the waiting area. He called us, and tech patched us into their security cameras. You should have seen her. She looked like a kid. She sat leaned over with her hands between her knees. Her head was down, eyes closed, like she was a little praying angel. Her face was all puffy like she'd been crying. Broke my heart."

"She's eighteen," Seth said. He looked around the room for his pants. Seeing the Bluetooth headset Ava called his "fallopian tube" on the table, he stuck it in his ear. "Legally an adult."

"It's hard to imagine. . ."

"I know." Around the time the fallopian tube connected to his phone, he found his pants near the door.

"Anyway, she got up to get a coffee from one of those places near the escalators at the entrance to the concourse. Harry thought he'd bag her out there where there were less people around," Ferg said. "But they play the televisions in the hallway. Harry was walking behind her when she stopped short at a TV. Harry almost ran into her."

"She saw her mom and sisters?" Seth set the phone

next to the bar sink and put on his pants.

"She saw them getting on the helicopter to come here," Ferg said. "The poor kid. She started bawling. Just right there. Harry asked her if he could help, and she said she needed to find a policeman. Harry is a policeman, so . . ."

"What did she say?" Seth looked around the room for his holster and shirt.

"She said that she had done something terrible because her mother and sisters were being held hostage," Ferg said.

"Where is she now?" Seth found his T-shirt near the bed.

"Safe," Ferg said. "Harry's with her. He told her that he would stay with her. He already called his sister to have her come in as Hillary's attorney. But Seth, the girl's a wreck. She wants to see her mom and sisters. They're at Denver Health. I told them I'd ask you . . ."

"It's a good idea." Seth saw his holster and handgun hanging on the desk chair. "If she knows they're really safe, she can tell us what she knows."

"I'll tell Harry," Ferg said.

"Do you know if the coroner got to the autopsy on Hillery Bloom, Jr.?" Seth asked. "Hang on."

Seth pulled his T-shirt on and slipped on his holster.

"Sorry, I missed that," Seth said. "I'm getting dressed."

"You asked about Grandpa Bloom?" Ferg asked. "Yep, the coroner said she sent an email to your phone."

"With pictures?" Seth saw his dress shirt in a ball behind the bedside table under the curtains.

"No idea," Ferg said. "She asked me, if I talked to you, to tell you to check your email."

"Thanks for the update," Seth said. "And tell your son he did really good."

"I'm proud of him."

"You should be," Seth said. "It's the kind of job that sounds easy but takes a lot of finesse. It's really good work."

When Ferg hung up, Seth kneeled down to grab his dress shirt. The door to the room opened.

"Go," Ava ordered Clara into her crate. Her voice was tense. From his position behind the table next to the curtains, he could only see the side of her face.

"Where is he?" a man's voice asked.

Seth realized his phone was on the sink. He couldn't call for help if he wanted to.

"Who?" Ava asked.

"O'Malley."

Seth slipped his handgun from the holster.

"Who?" Ava worked her voice so that she sounded confused.

"Don't fuck with me," the man said. "He rented this room. I know, because Delores *told* me."

"Why do you care?" Ava asked. "You have a contract for me."

"He's on the list," the man said. "Oh, you'd better believe he's on the list."

"Listen . . ." Ava must have taken a step toward him, because there was a scuffle. Ava fell to the ground.

Their eyes caught under the bed. He shook his head and motioned for her to stay down.

"Hill," She mouthed and held up three fingers. He nodded.

"I don't want to do this," Hill-three said. "You don't have any idea what he'll do, or what he's capable of. You think you've rescued them. He will hunt them to the ends of the earth and kill them like dogs. The only way to stop him is to get O'Malley. That's what his phone message said, 'Get O'Malley.' This is the only way ... the only way ..."

With his handgun trained on the man, Seth slowly stood up.

"Your father's dead," Seth said.

Seth kept his voice even and his demeanor calm. Hill-three had worked himself up into such a state that any fast movement could mean death to himself or Ava.

"He's not dead. How can he be dead?" Hill-three waved the handgun in the air. "You're trying to trick me. But I won't be fooled. I won't be. Meldy, the girls, Hillary – they're depending on me, and I won't fail."

When Hill-three grit his teeth and pointed the handgun, Seth fired.

Twenty-nine

The bullet ripped a channel in Hill-three's forehead and lodged in the seam between the ceiling and the wall. The force from the shot knocked Hill-three back. He bounced off the wall and hopped to his feet.

"You stupid . . ."

Blood from the wound on his forehead dripped into Hill-three's right eye. Like any rural person, when he felt the moisture on his forehead, he automatically wiped the blood with his hand. When his hand moved in front of his eyes, Hill-three noticed the blood. The man weaved forward, only to catch himself, and then weaved backward. Blood dripped down his cheek, onto his shoulder, and onto the carpet with every movement. Hill-three's eyes fixated on one blood spot and then another. He steadied himself and took a step forward. Seth gestured with his hand for Ava to stay down.

"You can't trick me, O'Malley. My father . . ."

Hill-three caught sight of a pool of his own blood and crumpled to the ground.

"What was that?" Ava asked.

"He faints at the sight of blood," Seth said.

There was a tap at the door.

"Everything okay in there?" Delores's voice came from the door. "Should I call the sheriff?"

"We're okay," Seth said. "Give us ten minutes and then call the sheriff. See if you can get Jimmy and your husband. He'll need someone he knows, and we need someone we can trust."

"Will do," Delores said. "Is he dead?"

"We're all breathing here," Ava said.

"Hill-three is wounded," Seth said. "It'll leave a scar, but that's all."

"Good," Delores said. "I'll come back with ice after I call."

Seth set his handgun on the table and went around the bed to Ava. He helped her up and held her close. Her body trembled, but she didn't cry. He kissed her neck.

"Shall we?" he whispered.

"Yes." With her head against his shoulder, she nodded.

He kissed the top of her head and went into the bathroom for towels. When he returned, Ava had turned Hill-three onto his side and taken a look at his cut.

"It's not bad," Ava said. "Did you plan on doing

that?"

"Sure," Seth smiled.

"Sure?"

"I've learned to always say I planned the random-assed things that turn out well," Seth said. "It's part of the magic."

Ava laughed.

"I wanted to wound him," Seth gave her a towel. "Make him bleed."

"This is a pretty good job," Ava smiled.

"I need to check my email," Seth said. "Can you take care of . . . that?"

"Sure," Ava mopped up the worst of Hill-three's wound. She took Hill-three's handgun and gave it to Seth. "What are you getting?"

"Ferg said the coroner sent me . . ." Seth's voice faded out. "Hmm."

"Ok, he's coming around," Ava said. "Mr. Bloom?"

Seth pointed Hill-three's handgun at its groggy owner.

"What . . .?" His eyes focused on Ava.

"I'm Amelie Alvin," Ava said. "This is Seth O'Malley. I believe you came to kill us."

Hill-three looked up at Seth, who smiled, and then back at Ava.

"Do you remember that?" Seth asked.

Hill-three nodded.

"You have a cut on your head," Seth said. "You'll need a few stitches, but it doesn't appear to be serious."

Ava helped Hill-three to sit up and gave him a

towel to press against his head wound.

"Are you going to kill me?" Hill-three whispered.

"Hadn't planned on it," Seth said. "Ava?"

"Maybe later," Ava said. "I'm not wearing the proper shoes."

Hill-three smiled at her irreverent tone.

"What happens now?" Hill-three asked.

"We have a couple of questions," Seth said. "I want to show you something. Then the sheriffs will escort you to Denver to see your wife and girls."

"They're okay?" Hill-three asked.

"They're alive," Seth said.

"It will take some time, but I think they'll be fine," Ava smiled. "Would you like to speak to them before you go?"

Hill-three nodded.

"Let's take care of a few things first," Seth said. "Your father is dead."

"Impossible," Hill-three shook his head. Seth nodded.

"I have a picture here of him on the coroner's table," Seth said. "Can you look at it and not pass out?"

"It's only blood," Hill-three said.

Seth passed his phone to Hill-three. He took a look at the photo, hiccupped, and began to cry.

"Is that your father?" Seth asked.

Hill-three nodded.

"You'll see that your father was shot in the head," Seth pushed the button on his phone so another photo came up.

"Who? You?" Hill-three asked.

"He was shot while in the commission of an attempted murder," Seth said. "Éowyn Alvin."

"I got a message from him," Hill-three's hands moved toward his pockets.

"Slowly," Seth gestured with the handgun.

Hill-three took a phone from his pocket.

"Give it to Ava," Seth said.

Ava took the phone and looked at it.

"What's the code?" Ava asked.

"081573," Hill-three's eyes filled with tears. "Phillip's birthday."

Ava listened to the message from Hillery Jr. She pressed some buttons and listened again.

"The message was recorded early this morning," Ava said. "But wasn't delivered until this afternoon."

"Probably when they moved the body to Denver," Seth said.

"I'm sure you're right," Ava said. "We always have trouble with cell service when we're up at the ranch."

"He's really dead?" Hill-three leaned back against the motel room door. "Wow."

Unsure of what Hill-three would do, Seth and Ava stood very still and watched.

"Sorry for trying to kill you," Hill-three gave a partial smile.

"We have a couple of questions," Seth said.

Hill-three nodded.

"Your father," Seth said. "He ran the murder-for-hire business?"

"When we were kids, he and Grampa would leave for the summer," Hill-three said. "When we got older, they would take us with them. Howie and I would hang out; go to museums . . . We had no idea."

Hill-three shook his head.

"No idea," Hill-three repeated.

"When did you find out?" Seth asked.

"Mom found out," Hill-three said. "Howie and me, we got home from school one day, and she was furious. I've never seen her so mad. She was the sweetest, nicest person you could ever meet, but not that day. She'd been in town, and the postal clerk had told her that Dad's mail box was overflowing. She had no idea he even had a mailbox. She went right away and . . ."

"Discovered what he was up to," Seth said.

"She was livid," Hill-three said. "She thought we knew, Howie and me."

"She didn't go with you on your trips?" Ava asked.

"No," Hill-three said. "Ranch life is hard, especially for women. There's so much work all the time and . . . She used the weeks we were gone to go to quilting retreats, deep clean the house, or just sleep. When we'd get back, she'd be rested and happy to see us."

"Did your father kill your mother?" Seth asked.

"We were there," Hill-three said. "He did it right in front of us. He told us we needed to harden up to take over the family business, but I . . . and Howie, he . . . It was all about the land, and we didn't give a crap about the land. I wanted to be a teacher. I love science. And Howie, he was brilliant – so smart. He wanted to change the world."

"And the killing?" Seth asked.

Hill-three squinted at Seth and then glanced at Ava.

"You're sure he's dead?" Hill-three asked.

Seth flicked his phone a bit and held it up again.

"That's an MRI of his brain," Seth said.

"Oh," Hill-three said. "It doesn't look quite right."

"He had severe lead poisoning," Seth said. "Probably as a child. His brain is riddled with scars and damage from it. Of course, the bullet made a mess."

"He's really dead," Hill-three said. "Wow."

"This, right here?" Seth pointed to an area in the middle of his brain. "That's brain cancer."

"Lead poisoning enhances antisocial tendencies," Ava looked at Seth. He nodded. "The cancer is in an area that would reduce his ability to make good decisions. Can I see it?"

Seth gave her the phone.

"This kind of cancer grows really fast," Ava said. "It would impair his judgment," Ava's voice indicated that it should be obvious. Seth looked at Hill-three and he shrugged. "He'd have become more irritable, angry, and irrational. You must have noticed that."

"I got sick last school year, really sick. The docs said I couldn't work anymore so we decided to move so I could get treatment. We were supposed to all live together – me and Phillip and Meldy and the kids, in Albuquerque," Hill-three said. "Dad didn't like it, but he accepted that was what had to happen. He was getting too old to live at the ranch and … Dad was going to live in the apartment over the garage. Then, Phillip showed up with his brother one day and . . . all hell broke loose. So, yeah, I noticed when he became more irritable and irrational."

Seth nodded.

"He didn't grow up on the Houghton Ranch, your Mom's ranch, did he?" Seth asked.

"No," Hill-three said. "He grew up on a ranch where the Army Maneuver Site is now. The Army used imminent domain to take the ranch. They got paid but . . . 'Some hurts, you never get over.' That's what my grandfather used to say."

"I saw a report that parts of the Maneuver area were riddled with lead from old mining claims," Seth said.

"Can we get it?" Ava asked. "They'll need it for their defense."

"I'll ask when we're done," Seth smiled at her kindness and turned back to Hill-three. "You wouldn't have been like your father or grandfather."

"We weren't," Hill-three said. "They tried to toughen us up, but Howie and me, we . . . weren't like them. We were such a disappointment to our father. But Mom, she was great, really great. She went behind Dad's back to set up her will like that. We got the land; he didn't. She loved us, sure – she was our mom. But she really liked us as people. It made having a weird dad all right."

"Why did he kill Howie?" Seth asked.

THIRTY

"Howie was going to sell," Hill-three said. "I was living in town and working at the high school by then. I hadn't really lived at the ranch since Mom had died. I was willing to keep a piece of my land so that Dad could live there. We were going to sell the rest. Dad always blamed Howie for everything, mostly because he got away. But Howie had Meldy. Together, they could do anything. So Dad killed him."

"How do you know?" Seth asked.

"He told me," Hill-three said. "Proved it with pictures. Then he found out that Meldy inherited the land. That's when Dad went totally crazy. He told me he would kill her and the kids if I didn't marry her. 'Keep the land in the family,' he said. I know it sounds stupid, but you don't know what he could be like."

"You'd also seen him kill your mother," Ava said.

"Your brother," Seth said.

"I love those kids," Hill-three said. "I'll never have kids of my own. Howie and Meldy always shared them like they were mine, too. And they're amazing girls, so sweet and smart. Meldy and those girls were my brother's whole world. Mine too. I had to do something to . . ."

Hill-three shrugged.

"Why did Meldy go along?" Ava asked.

"My dad put the fear of God into her," Hill-three said. "She had control of his land and . . . She was absolutely terrified of him. She married me and took that job in Albuquerque. We practically grew up together. It wasn't hard to pretend to be in love, not for either of us. We love each other. We're a family."

"How many people have you killed?" Seth asked.

They heard sirens in the distance coming in their direction.

"None. I was supposed to kill you." He pointed to Seth. "And you." He pointed to Ava. "You can see how well that went."

"And my mom? Vivian Alvin?" Ava asked.

"I was supposed to kill her too, but I saw Meldy being released," Hill-three said. "On the television. I saw it, so I figured it was all over, but then I got that message and . . ."

Hill-three shook his head.

"No sir," Hill-three said. "I haven't ever had the stomach for the family business. My brother neither. The truth is that I've always been sickly. I've never been very strong. I used to make jokes about it or pretend to make it happen, but I'd just get sick. Damned inbreeding in this stupid valley. I've spent a lot of time in hospitals. It's what interested me in science in the first place."

"And your daughter?" Seth asked.

"Hillary, oh God, poor Hillary." Hill-three sobbed into his hands. Ava put her hand on his shoulder to steady him.

"They're going to be here any minute," Seth said.

Hill-three nodded.

"What happened to Hillary?" Seth asked.

"When he freaked out and killed Phillip, he didn't remember anything about moving, nothing. He declared that we'd all stay there and he'd train Hillary to take his place, but she . . . she's just a sweet girl. She called me after . . . She was hysterical. I thought she'd kill herself, throw herself off the building. I think she would have if her mother hadn't been held hostage, and her sisters. You know what he made her do?"

Seth nodded.

"Someone beat Meldy really badly," Ava said. "The young girls were assaulted. Was that you?"

"No way," Hill-three said. "But I was there. Hillary too. He tied us up, too – made us watch. He killed Phillip and his brother in front of all of us. Ground up their bodies and . . . We were horrified, absolutely out of our minds with terror."

Hill-three dropped his head.

"You don't know what he's like," Hill-three's voice

was a whisper.

"Why make the Army wait until August to take possession of the land?" Seth asked.

"Hillary is a counselor at summer camp," Hill-three said. "We wanted to let the kids have one last summer in the valley before moving to Albuquerque. Of course, they went to move Howie right after school was out and Dad caught them. He dragged Hillary and me to the cabin and started . . ."

Fat tears rolled down Hill-three's blood stained cheeks.

"Hill-three?" Delores's voice came from the door. "Seth? Ava? The sheriffs are almost here. Can I come in? I have ice."

"One more question," Seth asked.

Hill-three looked up at him.

"Phillip was your lover?" Seth asked.

"How did you know?" Hill-three asked.

"Only closeted gay guys brag about how many women they've bagged," Seth said. "Even in high school."

"That's me – closeted, gay man," Hill-three nodded. "I thought I could cover it up. Meldy, she was so kind and loving, but she's never going to love anyone other than Howie. She wanted me to be happy. And our kids didn't care. I met Phillip through her. She pretended he was her lover, so I . . . so I . . . We were going to sell the land and live in Albuquerque all together. We're a family, a real family, and my Dad even agreed. He agreed. But then like a switch, he forgot everything and . . . and . . ."

"Seth?" Sheriff Jimmy Thatcher's voice came from

the door. "We're going to break down the door if you don't open it. That's a big expense for the hotel. You . . ."

"You ready?" Seth asked.

Hill-three nodded and Seth went to open the door.

"Thanks for coming," Seth said. "He needs to see a doctor. I'd like it if you and Deputy Robinson took him to Denver to see his wife and kids."

"He's not under arrest?" Jimmy asked.

"Protective custody," Seth said. "We don't really know who's behind all of this, so I'd appreciate it if you handle the situation carefully."

"Didn't he try to kill you?" Jimmy asked.

"I was just reminding a friend about hand grenades and horseshoes," Seth smiled. "This is one of those cases where *almost* doesn't really count. Ava?"

"He's been through enough, Deputy Thatcher," Ava said. "It's time to let this family heal."

Deputy Thatcher nodded and came into the room. For the next couple of hours, Seth and Ava stood to the side while the Las Animas County sheriffs worked the crime scene. Around midnight, they were released to go with a warning to be available if they were needed.

"Home?" Seth asked.

Ava nodded. They packed up their few belongings and grabbed Clara. They stopped for gas and coffee and hit the highway.

"So that's it," Ava said.

"That's it," Seth said.

"Can you explain it?" Ava asked.

"Sure," Seth said. "Once upon a time, a

Confederate assassin named Hillery Bloom moved to the Piñon Valley."

"Once upon a time?"

"I don't know the exact date," Seth said. "Sometime before 1913."

"Okay. Go on," Ava said.

"The problem with this ranch is that the water was contaminated with lead and probably other heavy metals," Seth said. "As you know, heavy doses of lead cause antisocial behavior. Although, given that this guy was a Confederate assassin, there wasn't far to swing. Just before the Great Blizzard of 1913 hit, a tax man named Paul Bradley came to talk to them about paying property taxes. The Confederate assassin killed the tax man, but not before fixating on an important bit of information – the state of Colorado didn't care how they got the money to pay their taxes. I can almost hear Paul Bradley saying, 'I don't care if you kill to get the money; you're going to pay your taxes on this land.'"

"Ooooh," Ava said. "Bad words of advice for an assassin. You sure?"

"Evelyn found something in the old records that all of the tax agents said something like that. It was a tough time. The state was floundering and really needed the money."

"It seems kind of reckless," Ava said.

"It was the wild, wild West," Seth said.

"Hmm," Ava said. "Go on."

"Hillery Bloom must have been a very literal person, because he took the tax agent at his word. He started killing people to pay his taxes. Hillery Bloom beget Hillery Bloom Jr. or, as I like to think of him, Gramps, late in life. Gramps goes with his pappy on killing adventures around the country. The number of murders equals the amount of money they needed for property taxes."

"Ok, that's just weird," Ava said.

"Weird is a word for it," Seth said. "Gramps married the lovely Mrs. Houghton-Bloom and moved to the Houghton family ranch on the north side of the valley. At some point, Hillery Bloom retires from the murder-for-hire business and Gramps takes over. Eventually, the lead-filled Bloom ranch is imminent domained by the Army, lots of pent up frustration, yada, yada, yada."

"I always like the yada-yada parts," Ava smiled.

"I know you do," Seth said. "Gramps continues to make the tax money by murdering people. When he has two sons, also later in life, he figures they will follow him into the business of murder."

"But they don't," Ava said.

"They aren't the type. Maybe it's the lack of lead in the water or a mother's love or just random genetics," Seth said. "But those boys are not murderers. Gramps kills their mother and Howie, and keeps up the land and family business. Come last fall, Hill-three is sick again. Hill-three and Meldy decide to sell the land and live in town. Gramps realizes the game is up and agrees. The girls are in school, so they wait out the school year. Phillip and his brother come for a visit, probably to see Hillary graduate, and Gramps loses it."

"Cancer takes over his brain and he forgets his

agreement," Ava said.

"Right," Seth said. "He does a lot of horrible things."

"With that type of cancer, he could have easily forgotten everything and gotten fixated on something," Ava said. "Like the land."

"Right. He'd lost a ranch to the Army. He wasn't about to let that happen again."

Ava smiled.

"He took this big contract, we have to assume, in order to buy the land from Hill-three and Meldy," Seth said.

"Or buy it back from the Army," Ava said.

"Maybe, but remember Hill-three said he didn't remember anything," Seth said. "It's more likely that he was trying to buy it from Meldy and Hill-three."

"And the fracking?"

"Hill-three and Meldy had already sold the ranch to the Army. Gramps had to do something to make the land unusable. There was nothing Hill-three or Meldy could do to stop him."

"That's almost a kind of brilliant madness," Ava said.

"In a psychopathic way," Seth said.

"There's also the problem of getting someone to take his place in the murder-for-hire tax payment plan."

"Right. He'd probably spent the last forty years mulling over what to do. Once the cancer sets in, his obsession returns. He kills off the lover, kidnaps the 'cause of all his problems' . . ."

"Meldy and the girls."

"Right," Seth said. "Tries to toughen everyone up and get the oldest granddaughter, Hillary, to take his place in the family business."

"Which she does."

"Which she's forced to do," Seth said. "I doubt any court will convict her."

"I agree," Ava said.

"Gramps kills Bella and your father with the experimental guided bullets he stole using Meldy's access," Seth said. "Hillary kills the marshals. Gramps goes after Éowyn and is killed by Switch. Hill-three is supposed to kill your mom, but leaves before he gets a shot off. In the car, he hears a voice message, delayed by the Grant County cellular gloom, and comes to kill us."

"Good job," Ava said. "You found the men responsible for your friend's unsolved mystery and got a killer off the streets. Will you tell McGinty?"

"After I sleep," Seth said. "There are a few unresolved details."

"Like what?"

"Like how Hill-three got to Trinidad in under five hours," Seth said.

"Plane ride to Denver; car to Trinidad," Ava said.

"How did you know?"

"I heard the sheriffs talking," Ava said.

Seth laughed.

"What else?" Ava asked.

"Where are the horses?" Seth asked. "Delores said they kept horses there."

"I know the answer to that too," Ava said. "Since they didn't live there after Mrs. Bloom died, they sold the stock to Meldy's cousin."

"And Gramps didn't mind?"

"He didn't care about horses," Ava said. "Or that's what Jimmy said when I asked him. Horses are a Houghton and Thatcher thing, not a Bloom thing."

"Ah," Seth said. "A Houghton and Thatcher thing."

"Anything else I can help the great detective with?" Ava smirked.

"Why did Meldy sell when Howie is buried on the land?" Seth asked.

"Well, that *is* interesting," Ava said. "That's actually one of the reasons I was in the cabin so long. Turns out Howie was cremated. His remains were placed at his favorite place on the land."

"The cabin?" Seth asked.

"The cabin," Ava said.

"That's what Hill-three meant when he said, they went to get Howie," Seth said. "Makes sense. Gramps captured them there rather than hauled them there. I wondered how he pulled that off by himself."

"Right. He killed Phillip and the brother there."

"And ground them up?" Seth asked.

"There," Ava said. "He put them in the garden beds because..." Ava shrugged.

"He's a madman?" Seth asked.

"Something like that."

"Thanks," Seth said.

"You bet," Ava smiled. "Who do you think was behind the contract on my family?"

"I don't think we'll ever know," Seth said.

"Will they come for . . . us?"

"I doubt it," Seth said.

"Why?"

"Because your father is dead. He was the real target," Seth said. "But I can ask around if you'd like."

"I'd like that," Ava said.

Seth glanced at her and smiled. She reached over to hold his hand. They lapsed into comfortable silence. After a few miles, Ava laid her head on his lap and fell asleep.

Seth kept his speed steady as he drove through Pueblo on I-25. With each passing mile, he knew he was driving closer to the moment when Ava would leave.

He ran scenarios in his head. Every possibility ended with her leaving for good. He thought about stopping the car just to get another few hours with her. But Seth was never one to avoid his fate. He slowed through Colorado Springs, but got back up to highway speed for the rest of the trip to Denver. He pulled up to his father's house around five in the morning. Although it was still dark, the light of sunrise had begun to peek at the edge of the horizon.

"We're here," Seth touched her back.

She sat up. Her eyes were red and swollen as if she'd been crying. She didn't speak, so he didn't either. He gave her a soft smile and drove into the garage. He held her hand as they walked through the backyard and into the house. He sat on the bed while she packed a small bag with her belongings. He held her hand and walked her to the back door. They stood, unspeaking, at the door for a long time. Finally, she smiled and kissed his lips.

As if her kiss had unlocked his frozen tongue, he said, "I love you."

She closed her eyes as if he'd stabbed her. Nodding, she took a breath and went to the garage.

"What was that?" Maresol asked from the doorway to the kitchen.

"Ava's leaving. For good."

Under Maresol's worried eyes, he walked up to his bedroom. He stripped off his clothing and took a shower. Because he never slept much when he was working on a case, he usually slept for at least a day when it was all over.

There was nothing he could do about Ava. The only thing he could do now was sleep. Maybe when he woke, he would figure out what to do next. But at this moment, he saw his entire life grind to a complete halt.

He got into bed naked and fell into a deep sleep.

|-||-|||-||-|||-||-|||-||-|||-||-|||-||-|||-||-|||

Thirty-one

"Papa."

The sound broke into Seth's deep sleep.

"Pa-pa-pa-pa-pa-pa," a small child's voice said.

The child squealed, and he felt the bed move. He opened his eyes to see his granddaughter Rachel crawling across the bed toward him.

"Pa-pa-pa-pa-pa-pa-pa-pa," she said and laughed. She reached a sticky hand out to him. He closed his eyes.

"Papa?" Rachel's voice sounded confused and a little sad.

He opened his eyes.

"Papa!" the child laughed.

"She's been saying that for days," Sandy's voice came from the end of the bed. He rolled over to look at her.

"We weren't sure what she was saying. Aden thought maybe she was calling him Papa."

The thought of her husband and Rachel's father made Sandy smile.

"She was very offended, because he's clearly Dada," Sandy smiled. "Finally, the great mystery has been solved."

Seth laughed. He shifted so that his back was against the head board. He situated the covers and pulled the baby onto his lap. She sucked her thumb and cuddled next to him.

"She seems to know when you're hurting," Sandy said.

"Ava's gone," Seth said.

Sandy sat on the bed next to him.

"I've always thought the whole thing was unlikely," Seth said. "She's got so much life in front of her, and I . . ."

"Feeling sorry for yourself? That's really not like you."

"Just stating the facts."

"Ah, the facts," Sandy raised her eyebrows. "Delphie told me you would marry three times."

Seth groaned. Undeterred, Sandy continued on.

"One to take care of. I assume that's crazy Emily."

Seth closed his eyes.

"Two for fun. That's got to be Bonita."

"God, Delphie can drive me absolutely crazy," Seth said.

"Don't interrupt," Sandy mock scolded. "And the third time for love."

"What about Andy?" Seth asked.

"That's what I asked," Sandy said. "What about my mother?"

"And the great oracle said?"

"Some loves have no beginning, no end, no formal ties, and no documents – only love," Sandy said, her eyebrows raised in a "How's that for an answer" look.

"I should sleep," Seth said.

"Well, you can't sleep," Sandy smiled. "I was sent up here with strict orders to cut your *shaggy* hair, shave your *scraggly* face, and help you get ready."

"For what?"

"Your wedding," Sandy said.

"Ava's gone." Seth's irritated response made Sandy smile.

"She left here early this morning," Sandy said. "She drove out I-70 and got on the 25. She thought she'd go to see her Mom or head to Fort Collins to reminisce about college days or whatever. She didn't count on the traffic."

"She works nights," Seth said. "I doubt she's ever seen the traffic that time of day."

"That's what she said. It took her an hour to get from your house to Eighty-Fourth," Sandy smiled. "She decided to wait out the traffic. So she went to the breakfast place right there. Anyway, she was there about a half hour when Dale showed up."

"Dale?" Seth asked.

"Shush," Sandy said. "It's a good story. Let me finish."

Seth nodded.

"Dale sat down and ordered breakfast," Sandy said.

"Ava said they didn't talk during breakfast. Not a word. When it was time to go, Dale said, 'You coming?' and Ava came home."

"But she wanted to find herself," Seth said.

"Sitting in the breakfast place, she realized that you were right," Sandy said. "She found herself through loving you. By driving away from you and your life together, she was driving away from herself, not closer to herself. She thinks she was mostly scared and very tired. So she came home."

"Papa," Rachel put her hand on his bare chest.

"Rachel," Seth kissed her cheeks. The baby laughed and waved her arms around.

"Delphie and Maresol were here when she got home," Sandy said. "I guess Maresol called Delphie the moment Ava left, which is how Dale got to the breakfast place. They told her not to wake you and to rest while they got everything ready. I woke her up a couple of hours later and it's been . . . Well, you know how it is."

"A lot of work," Seth said.

"A lot of work," Sandy smiled. "Anyway, you have about forty minutes to get dressed. Go shower. I'll cut your hair here and give you a shave. Maresol had your tux ironed. It's . . . uh . . . Watch Rachel for a minute."

Sandy trotted out of the room. She returned with Seth's tux. She hung the tux on the closet door and then left for his shoes. Seth heard Maresol yell from downstairs.

"What's going on?" Seth asked.

"Lizzy and Maresol," Sandy said. "Oh the drama."

Seth's laugh made Sandy laugh.

"Anything I should worry about?" Seth asked.

"If you're not out there in your tux in . . ." Sandy looked at her watch. "Thirty-seven minutes, you have a lot to worry about. Go shower."

"What?" Seth asked.

"Your bride is waiting for you," Sandy said.

"Ava?"

"Yes, Ava," Sandy said. "Would you prefer it if Maresol came up here to explain it to you?"

Grabbing the sheet and the baby, Seth jumped out of bed. He gave Rachel to Sandy.

"I have to see a man about a horse," Seth pointed to the bathroom.

"Well, don't be too long," Sandy said. "Or we'll be made into horse tamales."

Laughing, Seth closed the bathroom door.

|-||-|||-||-|||-||-|||-||-|||-||-|||-||-|||-||-||

Join us on the web!

You can find Seth and Ava on Facebook at:
Facebook.com/SethandAvaMysteries

Seth shares his Twitter account with Ava at :
twitter.com/SethOMalley

Many of the characters in the Seth and Ava Mysteries also appear in the Denver Cereal, sweet and crunchy serial fiction. Feel free to download your free eBook copy of The Denver Cereal, Volume One at CookStreetStore.com or where you purchase eBooks.

To learn more about Claudia Hall Christian, go to ClaudiaHallChristian.com, visit her on her blog: On-a-limb.com, or subscribe to her newsletter.

SethandAvaMysteries.com

ALSO BY CLAUDIA HALL CHRISTIAN

PAPERBACK – DENVER CEREAL SERIES: (Add s/h $4)

____ THE DENVER CEREAL: Invited to her ex-husband engagement party, Jillian Roper shows up in thigh high leather boots. ISBN: 978-0-9822746-4-4 $13.95

____ CELIA'S PUPPIES : The story continues as Celia's much loved people begin to face their demons. Life & love hang in the balance. ISBN: 978-0-9822746-5-1 $13.95

____ CASCADE : The never resolved past comes back to haunt Sandy & Delphie. Situations escalate to a final, startling resolution. ISBN: 978-0-9826417-0-5 $14.95

____ CIMARRON : The wreckage of everyone's lives gets worked through in simple and effective ways. ISBN: 978-0-9826417-9-8 $14.95

____ BLACK FOREST: A child serial killer turns everyone's lives upside down in an intense mystery. ISBN: 978-1-938057-00-7 $14.95

____ FAIRPLAY: A child serial killer turns everyone's lives upside down in an intense mystery. ISBN: 978-1-938057-04-5 $14.95

PAPERBACK – ALEX THE FEY SERIES: (Add s/h $4)

____ **The Fey** : Alexandra Hargreaves must reach past her pain, through memory, & beyond the grave to find her self & her future. ISBN: 978-0-9822746-3-7 $14.95

____ **Learning to Stand** : When a small child's life is in danger, Alex must muster the strength and courage to learn to stand again. ISBN: 978-0-9822746-8-2 $15.95

____ **Who I am** : Is Alex the Fey? As Alex grapples with doubt, her world fills with turmoil. ISBN: 978-0-9826417-2-9 $15.95

____ **Lean on Me** : With the help of friends, Alex & the Fey Team outsmart an attack on that threatens the world intelligence network. ISBN: 978-1-938057-02-1 $15.95

PAPERBACK – THE QUEEN OF COOL (Add s/h $4)

____ **The Queen of Cool**: After her husband's sudden death, Lo Downs discovers that she is penniless & trapped in the middle of a controversy involving a Weapon of Mass Destruction ISBN: 978-0-9826417-7-4 $15.95

PAPERBACK – SETH AND AVA MYSTERIES :(Add s/h $4)

____ **The Tax Assassin:** Seth and Ava are on the trail of an assassin who kills for the money to pay his land taxes. ISBN: 978-1-938057-08-3 $15.95

__ I'd like my books signed by the author + $1 Total: ____________

Name: ____

Address: ____

City, State, Zip code: ______________________________

Email: ______________________ Telephone:_ ____________

Make checks & money orders to:

Cook Street Publishing, PO Box 18217, Denver, CO 80218

eBooks available at CookStreetStore.com, Amazon, Barnes & Noble, & Smashwords